THE BROTHERHOOD OF GIANTS

by

Eric Carlton Neperud

For Piers, who brought amusement, creativity and humanity to fantasy.

By Eric Carlton Neperud

THE LIMBO CHRONICLES
- Trees And Weeds
- Limbo
- The Octagonal Knight
- Dragons And Golems
- The Brotherhood Of Giants
- Wizards And Druids

THE YELLOWSONE TRILOGY
- Wonders Of The Wilderness
- Fleas Upon Snow
- The Periphery Of Sorrow

ISBN: 978-0-9983838-4-2
ISBN-10: 0998383848
Published by Valhalla Books

Cover Illustration by Eric Carlton Neperud
Map on back cover by Eric Carlton Neperud
Map on page 187 by Eric Carlton Neperud

White-collar crime can be more devastating than blue-collar. I didn't believe that when I did my heinous acts, but I do now. Murder and rape is traumatic for the person involved, and their immediate family, but those kinds of crimes don't always infect a community. Taking the life savings of thousands of people, now that's a crime.

My name is George Seward. I was an accountant who embezzled millions of dollars from his clients' retirement accounts. Someone on the outside might say I did it because I never saw the people I hurt---they were just account numbers. But, you see, I did see their faces, most of them anyway, some nearly every day. The problem is, it didn't bother me to see their faces. Money is just a tool, and depriving them of a hammer or a wrench wasn't that bad, was it? It wasn't like I was hitting them on the head with it.

I was finally caught, as we all are who don't know when to stop. Clandestinely transferring funds from one account to another was my addiction. Like most addictions I became acclimated to the fix, needing more of the drug to get the same high. I got greedy and careless. It had become too easy. I no longer watched my back. I even offered the person who caught me a piece of the action. She declined---the nerve of that woman.

If I hadn't been so greedy I may have spent a year or two in a minimal security facility. Sadly, the number of people who I hurt mattered in the sentencing. I was to spend the remainder of my life in prison, specifically at Dartmoor Penal Colony, a penitentiary world populated exclusively by convicts. I hadn't done a day of hard labor in my life. To eke out an existence in the wilderness wasn't the type of challenge I looked forward to.

To put salt on the wound I was made to strip before I was forced through the transport portal. And not just down to my underwear. They wanted me to leave the civilized world the same way I entered it. Some people liked to show off their bodies. Someone 170 sims tall who weighed 150 kilos, didn't. I was one of those people who made you grimace when you thought of them wearing a bathing suit.

The portal wasn't constructed of the conventional polished metal I was accustomed to seeing. Its sheen made it look metallic, but it was of many colors, one transitioning to another fluidly. I wasn't the type of person who did something to eliminate it. I delayed the inevitable. It took me five minutes to travel the final five meters to the portal. I would have delayed even longer if that voice hadn't threatened me. Threatened was the precursor to being touched. I don't like being touched. That's the main reason I don't date women. At least that's what I say to myself when I am home alone.

Chapter 1

CROCODILE

Expecting to step unto a metal or concrete platform, I stumbled when my feet compacted spongy earth. A man my size isn't graceful, so I wasn't able to recover. I fell. The softness of the ground prevented any physical damage. Without an audience, the supplemental emotional scars were held to a minimum.

Where was everyone? Hundreds of thousands of people were sentenced to Dartmoor every year, millions of people over the more than a century of its operation. There should have been someone to great me. Was I just randomly dumped in this jungle?

The trees went on forever in every direction. Being accustomed to the structured setting of court and a jail cell, the crazed cacophony of animal sounds brought me to the brink of a mental breakdown. An accountant wasn't familiar with such chaos. Peace and quiet was what I craved.

The epiphany was abrupt and jarring: HOW WAS I TO SURVIVE?! I didn't cook. A hot meal for me was driving home fast enough from a drive-thru that my food didn't get cold. Or ordering the food by vid---with the camera turned off, of course. What sane person wanted their image electronically sent for others to view?

I never connected being sent to a penal wilderness with not having someone take care of me. No food and no place to stay? With what money will I pay rent? Will I have to build my own home?

Thinking of food made me hungry. Contemplating the lack of pre-packaged, prepared provisions, I began to panic. People ate nuts and berries in the woods. I think that's what they did when they went camping. A jungle should have fruit in it. I didn't see any bananas, or apples, or strawberries, or grapes. How long had it been since I ate something that wasn't fried? I like desserts---wasn't fruit supposed to be nature's candy?

I was also thirsty. At least there's water here, but it's not bottled, or even filtered. Don't people get sick drinking natural water? What a way to die: death by diarrhea. But if I didn't drink something soon I would probably die anyway.

A bog was within sight. I was so accustomed to living in a pampered society, I became perplexed, for a moment. How was I going to drink without a cup? I knelt down---which wasn't a problem. It's amazing how effective gravity is in helping a fat man get closer to the ground. The hard part would be getting back up. I expected the water to smell. Didn't swamps always smell? I expected mildew or rot. It smelled almost pleasant, like rose water. I thought about drinking directly from the source, but if I dipped my head that far down I feared I would tumble into the water. I cupped my hands instead. I thrust them into the murky water. Its temperature was comparable to the air: about 25 degrees. It was warm in the jungle, but not unbearable, even with the humidity. I brought my filled hands up to my mouth and drank. The water actually tasted good, like an herbal broth. Beef or chicken would have been better, but I'll take what I can get.

I thrust my hands back into the water. They never came back up. As they snapped off at the wrists, the impulse propelled what remained of me backwards. I was more shocked than in pain. That agony began when the crocodile started consuming the rest of me. I didn't mind too much at that point. What was a person to do without hands?

Chapter 2

NAGA

This is where the story becomes strange. I woke up with my body intact. Had a brilliant surgeon been sentenced to Dartmoor and reattached my hands? I felt very weak, and sore, but there wasn't a scratch on me, not even a scar. Where was the doctor? There still wasn't anyone around. Did he leave before I woke? Why would he do that? Was I not permitted to have human contact the initial days of my incarceration? Except under life and death situations? If someone hadn't intervened I would have died.

Having nothing better to do, I remained in a prone position. Some might call that being lazy. I considered it conserving my energy. And if I was to find food later I couldn't waste what little energy I had by standing on my feet.

"I always find it amazing how infants react to their surroundings on their first day, but your reaction is a new one." The voice came from above, up in the trees somewhere. "Aren't you going to at least see who I am? You didn't even lean up to see who might want to eat you."

"Why would a person want to eat me?"

"People aren't the only ones who talk on Limbo, infant."

"I've heard of animals mimicking human sounds, but they aren't supposed to be able to sustain a conversation."

A rustling was heard in the trees. Something was coming towards me---emerald green and elongated. It descended, extending from a branch above me. Its amber eyes stared at me. "Have you ever heard of a snake speaking?" Through hisses I heard human speech, in Esperanto, with a Rigelian accent. "You look dumbfounded."

I crawled away from the thing. Not being very efficient at it, I pushed myself up. I thought, in my fatigued state, the maneuver would be more difficult, but it was actually easier. Once up, I backed further away from the snake. Something wasn't right. I looked down at my legs. They appeared to be smaller. Did the doctor also do cosmetic surgery? I looked at my belly. It too was smaller.

"You're lazy *and* vain. I wouldn't admire myself if I looked like you. As you can see, I'm very narrow and sleek."

"But I was much larger just minutes ago. Or was it days? I don't know how long I was unconscious."

"Some mutations are beneficial. Gaea must have taxed you with a portion of your girth."

"Was she the doctor who operated on me?"

"In a sense. But when you left her operating room you were not just fixed, you were remade. You died and were re-created."

"Like what Hindu's believe?"

"Similar."

"And you were reincarnated into a snake?"

"Re-created. And those of us with serpent attributes wish to be called naga. To retain our attachment to the old world we borrow old world mythology. Some breeds prefer more modern terms: trogs instead of dwarves, arbols instead of elves."

"Could I one day be re-created as an elf?"

"You could be. Or, perhaps, an ogre. It depends on your morality when you die, and blind luck. But some people say with Gaea there is always a plan."

"Is Gaea the ruler of Dartmoor?"

"Locals call this world Limbo, because no one truly dies here. We live in perpetual transition from one physical form to another. Gaea is the mythical earth mother. It's just a name we attach to the unexplained, but there are some Limboans that believe Gaea is real, a living god."

"If Gaea can make me skinny, I'll bow down to her."

"Gaea isn't that type of god. She is more passive. She doesn't need, or want, worshipers."

"I'm George Seward."

"No, you're not. Once you begin your life on Limbo, your other life ends. The first person who finds you is the one who names you. You entered Limbo in the Weedwoods, so that's your surname, your family name. Your common name must be more unique, more representative of you. I like the wood theme. What's associated with wood that's mushy like you? Pulp. Your name from today until the end of days is Pulp Weedwood."

"I don't think I like that."

"I imagine you didn't always like George Seward, but that's the name that was given to you. We aren't the ones who choose our names, but we're the ones who must live with them."

"Can you help me find some food, and clothes?"

"I don't believe you'll want to eat what I eat. When our form changes so do our appetites. I suggest you head for Henriville or Teakton. Walk due east. You'll hit the coastal road eventually.

Either direction will take you somewhere."

"Which way is east? I was never very good at outdoor activities."

"In these parts sunward is slightly west of north. If you keep the sun on your left, you'll eventually hit the road."

"Doesn't the position of the sun change?"

The naga laughed, sounding like a leaky radiator. It didn't elaborate. It would have bothered me more if I hadn't been laughed at my entire life. I wasn't completely immune to ridicule, but I was desensitized: scratches and scrapes now, instead of punctures and lacerations.

"I guess this is goodbye then, Mr. Naga. When I'm skinny like you maybe I'll come back for a visit."

As I walked eastward I heard the naga mumble, "Maybe after a dozen re-creations."

Chapter 3

BREEZE

Being more aware of the dangers of Limbo, I only had a couple more noteworthy encounters.

The first was with a gorilla. It ran right at me. I had to lunge to one side in order to avoid contact with it. One doesn't lunge without falling over, at least when one was overweight. Which was fortunate, because I discovered the gorilla wasn't running towards me, but away from a bull. I would have been trampled to death. I stayed down, raising my head just enough to see the outcome of the inevitable demise of one of those beasts. The bull had a secret weapon. It released a roar that stunned the gorilla. Before it could recover, the bull blew out a green gas from its mouth and nostrils. When the gas finally dissipated the gorilla looked like a stone replica of itself. The bull walked up to its prey slowly, not like it was being cautious, but like the hard work was over so it could take it easy the rest of the day. It began chewing on the stone, crunching on it bit by bit, gradually making it disappear, like a chocolate bunny.

I backed away as hastily as my---lack of---athleticism permitted, keeping an eye on it in case it wanted a second course. Half the gorilla remained when I lost sight of it. I turned around and began walking even faster. With my decreased bulk I was able to move at an astonishing rate.

My second encounter caught me more by surprise. Something black dropped onto me. The beetle was enormous: larger than my fist. It landed on my back. Its small head burrowed into my flesh. I began to feel weak. I collapsed. Before I lost unconsciousness, I attempted to pry it off me, but reaching behind one's back wasn't easy, especially for a person my size.

I woke, again. I was as weak as last time, but not as sore. I expected to see the naga again. I didn't. Nothing spoke to me or dropped down from a tree. With civilization still kays away I immediately got up. It was even easier than last time. I looked down. I was male. It had been years since I could confirm that---from this orientation. My body had shrunk again. Gaea had suctioned off another 20 kilos.

If only I could die a few more times before I met anyone. No, I didn't seriously consider suicide. You might remember, I put things off as long as I could, including death. I already felt less apprehensive about meeting someone naked. How would I feel after another couple of re-creations?

I intersected a road an hour later, if you could call the

shallow trench running above the ocean a road. Inmates were apparently not permitted mechanized transportation. And I didn't see any signs of animals either. Did that mean people walked everywhere? What cruel and unusual punishment had I been subjected to?

I chose to head away from the sun. My rationale, the further I got from the sun, the cooler it was going to be. I preferred cooler weather. A man my size perspired profusely, and frequently.

It wasn't long after that that the sky darkened. The sun hadn't set or become obscured by clouds. The golden orb looked like it was dimming. I was on the verge of having a panic attack. Was the sun going nova? Would the planet gradually become too cold to support life, my own, in particular? I collected palm fronds while there was still enough light to do so. I dug a small burrow out of the sand atop the bluff and placed half of the fronds in it. I lay down and covered myself with the remaining fronds. It was more comforting than comfortable. I looked up at where the sun was minutes ago. A full moon had replaced it.

I tried to sleep. The crashing surf below drowned out most of the animal sounds from the jungle, but not enough of them for me not to be aware of their presence. I was exhausted. All that walking and being re-created twice, but I couldn't fall asleep. Maybe I was too tired. I've heard of that happening to people, but never to me.

I was almost asleep, half-conscious, half-dozing, when I heard, "May I share your camp with you?"

I assumed I was dreaming. I voice that sweet never talked to me when I was awake. I opened my eyes briefly, then re-shut them.

"It's safer together than alone. I'll sleep over here, so you can have your privacy. Just knowing someone is nearby will help. Good night."

I opened my eyes and sat up. I thought I saw someone's blue eyes shut. I must have been mistaken because the lids looked like they closed horizontally. I must have been dreaming.

I woke to the sounds---and smells---of cooking. Two fish roasted on wooden skewers over a fire. So, someone had joined me last night. I leaned up, looking around. I didn't see anyone. Had she abandoned me already? At least she left me breakfast. I was famished. I cautiously removed one of the skewers, careful not to burn myself, or lose the meat on it. I examined it---it looked edible---then pulled off a chunk of meat. It burned my fingers. I dropped it in the sand. I picked it up and carefully brushed off the granules. I plopped it into my mouth. It was the best thing I have ever tasted. I was more careful with my next piece. I blew on it before plucking it, then I blew on it again, before placing it in my mouth. I began to choke. Something was lodged in my throat. I coughed, first from reflex, then from self-preservation. Something small, dense, and elongated flew out of my mouth. Was that a bone? Connoisseurs believed natural fish to be more flavorful than cloned cells, depending on the contaminants, but to me, not worth the inflated price, and hazards.

Now that my primary need was taken care of, modesty became paramount. My camp companion may return any moment. I attempted to fashion a garment from my bed. The fronds were plenty big, but conjoining them would be a challenge.

"Using a vine might help," suggested the sweet voice from the previous night.

I was startled, but not enough to lose my grip on the fronds. I turned towards the voice. My hands couldn't retain their grip, exposing me completely. But from what I saw perhaps it didn't matter. The voice was attached to a female, but it wasn't human---most of it. It was the height of a woman, but it looked more like a cat. It had spotted orange fur like a jaguar. Its tail was nearly a meter long. The remainder of its features were a cross between human and feline. It had breasts, but they were smaller than what a typical human woman would have. The breasts reminded me of the fantasies I had about the woman who slept next to me. I shuddered.

"Or you could choose to wear nothing at all. I don't. I do have this wonderful natural coat that you don't have. It's what I like most about my re-creation. I don't mind that I haven't completely lost my femininity, either." I blushed. It wasn't often I saw a woman naked, even a pseudo one. Okay, never. Not in person. "And it looks like you don't mind either."

I picked back up the palm fronds, covering what I could, the best I could. "Don't be embarrassed. We on Limbo are more liberated about such things."

"Well, I haven't been here that long. It might take a while before I get used to them."

"Suit yourself. It's time for me to break my fast." The feline woman walked up to the remaining skewer and waved it around like she was dancing. Maybe I had been away from women too long, even from the distance I required. Her feline attributes became less pronounced and her human female ones more so.

I needed to focus on something else. "So where were you when I woke?"

"I had to defecate. I did so in private, away from camp. Felines are facetious in their hygiene. Which reminds me." She began washing herself, as cats do. It was fascinating until she reached certain areas. I finally had to turn away.

When the sound of a raspy tongue on fur stopped I turned around and asked, "Can you help me find other humans?"

"Humans aren't very fond of demons, what they call those who have mutated into non-human forms. They often hunt them for sport. Some, I guess, deserve it, but most of us don't. I'm walking towards Henriville, so we can travel together until we reach the outskirts. I'm returning to my home in Chanu."

My confused expression was rewarded with an explanation. "The Chaotic-Neutral Frontier." That didn't help. "Demons are clustered by morality. My kind, spotted felinoids, are Neutrally-

Chaotic. Our interaction with others is neither Positive nor Negative, and we tend to be inconsistent in the manner in which we act."

"Do you live there because of your actions, or because of your actions you live there?"

"When we are re-created we sometimes mutate. Well, we always mutate, but sometimes more extremely. Our mutations aren't entirely physical. Sometimes they're intellectual, or moral. If we have behaved ourselves since our last re-creation we are more likely to be re-created in the Positive Frontier. If we haven't, we're more likely to be re-created in the Negative. Being a penal colony, there are more Negative individuals here than Positive. The vastness of the Negative Frontier, in comparison to the Positive, is called the Moral Bulge. It should be more appropriately named, the Immoral Bulge."

"Because I entered Limbo near the Chaotic-Neutral Frontier, does that mean I am close to being Chaotic-Neutral?"

"Everyone enters Limbo in Neutrality. Because you entered near the frontier you *may* have Chaotic-Neutral tendencies. Neutral is Neutral until you show Gaea differently."

"But I always thought of myself as Ordered. I'm an accountant."

"Did you behave non-ordered in other aspects in your life?"

"If you're asking did I live a perfectly ordered life, being here answers that question. An ordered life doesn't include being sentenced to Limbo."

"The inconsistency of accounting and what got you here sounds like Chaos to me."

"You make me sound like one of those people who don't know what they want to do with their lives, so they wander from job to job, and from place to place."

"I don't see you doing any accounting work, and I'm sure this place was nothing like the place you grew up in."

"If I was interested in doing some accounting work, how

might I go about doing it? Have you heard of anyone hiring?"

"There may be a demand in some of the larger cities---in Gulag or Rhinopolis. Topiary may have a position, but that's 150 kays away, and you're too new to Limbo to make such a long journey. The Wizards might also have a need for accountants, but they don't like outsiders."

"Wizards?"

"Dealers in elem, elemental energy. They live in their keep near Gulag, in the Southern Spine. The terraforming residues that assist in our re-creation also created elem---pseudo-technology in a non-technological society. Certain effects are created when particular combinations of elem are combined."

"It sounds like chemistry. Mixing these *elem* precisely to get the desired effect must be complex? One wouldn't want to blow himself up by mistake."

"Being organized helps. Wizards rarely have these *accidents*. Rogue manipulators---warlocks and witches---are less likely to implement a systematic approach, resulting in greater casualties. Demons are often bestowed with innate abilities, so there isn't as great a desire, or need, for someone like me to handle elem."

"Keeping things organized sounds like accounting. Where might a person go to learn how to combine elem?"

"That would be the Wizard's Keep. It's rare for an individual to be granted permission to join their order. Because people never die on Limbo---permanently---there isn't much turnover. No one is allowed to leave the order. Those who have tried have been rumored to have been enclosed in stone for eternity."

"So, you wouldn't recommend me heading to Gulag one day?"

"Gulag? Yes. To the Wizard's Keep? No. If you truly wish to learn how to mix elem, seek a witch or warlock."

"I thought they weren't very good."

"Most of them. Those that still live---in their original form---

after a certain number of years, have apparently exceeded expectations."

"Is there one of these overachievers nearby?"

"There's a witch in the Herbal Islands. Her name is Manta. There's a small fishing fleet in Henriville. If you barter a few days of work, one might take you where you wish to go."

We had been walking half-an-hour, south, on the coastal road. Without preamble, the feline woman disappeared. A moment later I saw two men walk towards me, the first two humans I had seen since my incarceration. They were dressed in little more than loincloths. They carried huge backpacks, simple, but well-constructed. Their bare feet gently thudded on the soft earth.

"Good morning," said one of them, as the two kept walking. I moved out of their way. They had a heavier load than I. The other one simply shook his head after getting a good look at me.

"IS HENRIVILLE FAR?!" I shouted at them as they passed me.

"Four kays," the first one replied, his form already diminishing.

A couple of minutes later the feline woman returned. "Those freight-haulers looked determined, didn't they?" She shook her head. "Trading toil and tender feet for token trinkets? Becoming a demon, you're less likely to think about material things. It's about time I left you for good. The traffic is becoming atrocious. My name is Breeze Viola. Actually, Breeze Viola-by-the-Sea. Why couldn't I have entered Limbo in some place with a shorter name? Perhaps we'll meet again."

Breeze walked off into the jungle. As I watched her curves I couldn't think of many things better than hooking up with her again. Maybe I'll lose another 40 kilos by then, and mutate into something myself. Maybe into a dog. No, that just wouldn't be right.

Now that Breeze was gone my mind gravitated---most of it---to meeting others of my kind. How would I interact with them?

What would they think of me? They would probably think I needed to wear some clothes, but considering what the freight-haulers wore it didn't have to be much. I used a vine to tie palm fronds together, to form a kilt. I still didn't look like a model, but I had lost enough weight that going bare-chested no longer embarrassed me.

Chapter 4

SHELL

As I got closer to Henryville I began seeing more people. There were a couple of men who were harvesting fruit from an orchard, and a woman collecting reeds from a marsh. None of them were wearing more than was necessary to cover those areas of the body normally not seen. The men were the burly type that picked on me when I was young. I walked past them, trying not to look at them, pleading---internally---they reciprocate. They did. I liked nothing better than being inconspicuous. The best way to describe the woman, without being rude, was to call her plain. But it was easier talking to one of those women than one who was too pretty. I had trouble looking directly at the beautiful ones, and my words never came out right. "Where might a person find some less *natural* clothing?"

The woman looked up at me, attempted to retain her composure, but couldn't. Her grin erupted into a guffaw. Some men might find a woman laughing at them offensive, but considering most women ignored me, the greeting was perceived as her being gracious. Content in her prescience---bordering on being pleased---she became less plain. I almost thought of her as attractive now. “Sorry. It’s not often an infant comes up to me dressed in green diapers. My name is Shell Weedwood. The first time I saw the ocean was when I was dropped off here---almost this exact spot. I was fascinated with it---the water, the horizon, the seals, the seagulls, and especially, the shells. I should have spent more time being aware of my surroundings than looking at the pretty things beside my feet. Something thought *I* was just as pretty. I think it was a giant crab. Some things on Limbo are larger than we are accustomed to. I was eaten, but not entirely. I know this, because I was re-created a kay down the beach. I am one of the few people who have actually seen their own corpse, parts of it anyway. I have died two more times, but have always been re-created within a kay of my arrival on Limbo. That’s probably why I don’t show any signs of mutation.”

“I have died twice so far. Both times happened shortly after I arrived.”

“It’s remarkable how many times that happens to infants. I guess we are in so much shock when we first arrive we aren’t very proficient in taking care of ourselves. Someone coined same-day death as infant mortality. I think of it more like an abortion, a life terminated before it really becomes a life.”

Talking to Shell made her more attractive. She didn’t have the exotic beauty of Breeze, but she was a real woman. I could see myself spending time with her. She wasn’t a fantasy.

“I’ll find some clothes for you. Someone helped me when I was an infant. It’s time I returned the favor. Many men tried to help me when I first arrived. They consider new arrivals virgins. In some ways, I guess we all are. There are five times as many men as women. Some of the men have turned to other men to fill their needs. Some take what they want. Most barter. A woman is a valuable commodity. Choosing not to share that commodity is also valuable. It gains respect. I’m considered a member of the community. Some of the other women are just chattel. I have given in once...possibly twice. Women are most valued when they first arrive, and after they are re-created. That house you see up the hill was the product of one bartering session."

I didn't know how to react to Shell's statements. She was innocent, but not. Definitely less innocent than I, socially anyway. "Help me carry those reeds to the house. I make baskets with them. One's body isn't the only commodity to barter."

Shell loaded my outstretched arms with the meter-long reeds. After she grabbed an armful herself she headed up the hill. I followed her

Her house may have been a shack, but its wooden walls were sturdy. It had two rooms. The lower level had a wooden table bounded by two benches, an additional bench---padded with dried palm fronds---against a wall, two chairs, and a stone stove. The upper story was a loft with a small wooden nightstand, a wardrobe---essentlally shelves---and a wooden frame bed with fronds padding a reed mesh. In one corner of the lower level was a pile of reeds. "Drop them here," Shell said after dropping hers. She climbed up the ladder to the loft.

A small window was cut out of every wall. There was a good view of the sea through the one on the same side of the house as the door. I could only see jungle through the other three.

Shell climbed down the ladder with a cotton shirt and shorts. "Let's see if they fit."

I frowned. Unless...THEY STRETCHED! I looked around, hoping to find a dressing room or perhaps a bathroom.

Shell blushed. "I'll turn around."

My makeshift shorts wouldn't budge. I had tied the vine too tightly. It was embedded in my less substantial, but still substantial gut. I tried to untie the knot. It also wouldn't cooperate. I gave up, putting the cotton shorts on underneath. Then I pulled the shirt over my head. "Done."

She turned around and laughed. Was I in a dream? I had been given significant attention from a beautiful woman *twice* in one day. "I got a knife somewhere. Let me cut off those fronds for you." Beside the stove she picked up a roughly forged knife with a wooden handle.

As she approached to cut the vine, I backed away. "I better do that." She turned the knife around, handed it to me at its tip. I was concerned about her cutting me, but even more concerned about her having to touch my gut to do so. As carefully as I could I squeezed the knife between my belly and the vine. I sliced away at the vegetation in a rocking motion. The frond kilt fell away.

Shell looked at me with a scrunched up face. I looked down. The shorts left little to the imagination. "I think we can find you some larger pants in town tomorrow. They don't look very comfortable."

"I'll manage." I tore away a couple of the palm fronds from the vine and stuck them into the top of the shorts. I bent them forward. They looked stupid, but less obscene. The compression to my gut---and its sudden release---did a number on me. "You wouldn't happen to have a bathroom, would you?"

"Plumping isn't prevalent on Limbo. Most men prefer to go in the woods. There's also an outhouse behind the house, back a ways. There should be some fronds in it. If not, you'll have to re-supply."

It was a surprisingly pleasant experience. The fronds took a while to get used to, but the small wooden shack was well ventilated, and with just one person using it odors hadn't accumulated. I imagined women's restrooms to be more like boutiques than locker rooms. The more refined gender had better aim and didn't have the compulsion to mark their territory. There were no lacy curtains or doilies or scented candles, but there was a nice view of the forest through the cracks in the cedar planks.

"What can I do to repay you for the clothes?" I asked after I returned.

She glanced over at the pile of reeds. "We need to come up with something to barter those new shorts of yours with." You would think that making baskets would be easy. I don't know if it was my inexperience, or my clumsiness. I never made a basket decent enough to sell. While I became increasingly frustrated Shell completed ten perfect ones.

"It will be dark soon. Take that bucket to the spring behind the hill and fill it with water?" I did as I was told. I had a honey-do list and I wasn't even married.

The sun was still in the same location it had been since I had arrived on Limbo. It was beginning to dim. I hurried to the top of the hill, pausing for a few seconds to take in the view. There wasn't any. The trees were full enough that the sea was completely obscured. I headed down the backside of the hill. About halfway down I found the spring. Water leaked out of a hole. It pooled beneath it, where the water had eroding the earth enough to expose granite. The pool was barely three meters across. The excess dribbled downhill, first as a 50-sim waterfall, then as a cascade. I sliced the edge of the bucket into the water. It quickly filled. I picked up the full bucket, but instead of heading back over the hill I went around it. It was much heavier full than empty.

I followed a trail that had almost been reclaimed by the forest. Someone was coming towards me. Actually, I was coming towards him. It didn't look like he was moving. As I got closer I realized it wasn't a he, but a what---a statue, red before the elements had emasculated its luster. I set the bucket down to examine it. I believed it to be constructed of stone, but upon touching it I learned it was made of clay. It looked human, but in a very rudimentary manner. Why would someone put a statue here?

I returned to Shell with the bucket of water. If it had gotten any darker I would have become lost. "What took you so long?" she asked. Shell was attractive, but not that attractive. She was finishing cutting up vegetables on the table. She added carrots, potatoes, and onions to the crabmeat already in the kettle. "Ever since I was attacked so viciously, crab soup has become my favorite." A fire blazed at the base of the oven. Shell poured the water into the kettle. She stirred it with a wooden ladle, added spices, then hung it on a metal dowel above the flames. On the stone outcropping above the stove lay six grain cakes.

"I found a clay statue." Shell's face lost its color. "I didn't do anything to it. I just touched it to verify what I saw. Is it yours? It seems an odd place to leave a statue."

Shell sat down in one of the chairs. Color was beginning to return to her face, but slowly. "No, it wasn't mine. It belonged to Salt. He arrived in Henriville ten years ago. Some of the stories he told about the west were amazing. He was friends with arbols and trogs and mer. He stayed with me for seven years. He would wander off doing odd jobs, fishing mostly, but sometimes he hauled freight. Eventually his wanderlust got the best of him. He left on a passenger ship and never returned."

"Why put a statue on the side of a hill?"

"It isn't a statue. Not originally. It was golem---a mechanized servant. Elem aero was its energy source. I never knew where Salt got his elem. He never told me. When he left so did the energy required to power the golem. While fetching water for me one day it stopped moving, its energy expired."

Shell didn't speak much the remainder of the evening. When the soup and grain cakes were done we ate them silently in the candlelight. Shell rolled out a reed mat for me and padded it with palm fronds. She wished me a goodnight, then climbed up the ladder to the loft.

In the morning Shell's demeanor had improved. She laughed once more at my frond stuffed shorts. After breakfast we traveled to town. I removed the fronds before I reached the settlement, my rationale being the hamlet was mostly male, and if they had never seen a bulge before they had bigger problems than a desire to make fun of me.

The people of Henriville were courteous. How much of that was due to me being accompanied by Shell? On the way to the general store we passed a building with painted images of nude women on its exterior. Shell sped up.

She sold the baskets for a copper each. Eight of them were spent buying the shorts, allowing her to pocket the other two.

I cohabitated with Shell for eight years. Eventually she shared her loft with me---and other things. I---initially---helped her make baskets. Yes, I did get better. But with making baskets we were barely earning enough money to sustain us. I still dreamed of being an elem accountant. But in order for me to do so I needed money. Seed money was necessary for any business. I thought about hauling freight, but even with my more fit physique---I didn't die again, but I was able to lose weight on my own, and actually build muscle---the desire for that much physical labor wasn't in me. I could farm or fish. The dynamics of fishing interested me more. It was easy finding a job on one of the fishing boats. Fishing was plentiful. Fishermen weren't. We must have fished every hectare of the southwest corner of the South Sea. Sometimes we even went as far north as Sage Island, or as far east as Oregano. We wandered into Chanu three or four times, but never into Chaneg---the Chaotic-Negative Frontier. We passed the witch's island a couple of times a year, but always from a distance. Few had the fondness for unsanctioned elem manipulation as I.

It was finally time to inform Shell of my long-term plans. I'd rather be torn apart by crocodiles. "But if you train with the witch you may never return," she began.

"It shouldn't take more than a year."

"You'll meet dozens of women."

"Probably just one. Spending time with her will make the return to you all the more desirable."

She didn't say much after that. What could she say? She knew I was leaving her, likely forever, like Salt did those many years ago. She should have been content with the time we spent together. Most marriages didn't last past the initial three-year contract.

When I woke the day I was to leave, Shell wasn't beside me in bed. She wasn't even in the cabin. If she wasn't present when I left how could I leave her? Semantics, yes, but it must have made a difference.

Chapter 5

MANTA

One of the fishing boats I occasionally worked on agreed to carry me to the witch's isle. It was officially named Curry Island, but no one ever called it that. The 1000-hectare protrusion of stone was just three kays from Chaneg. It was rumored to be moving closer to it every year. That meant either the island was moving or the frontier. Neither scenario gave me much comfort. The island didn't have a harbor, so I was rowed to its sole narrow beach. "THANK YOU!" I yelled back to the captain as the dingy hastily returned to the ship.

"JUST DON'T TRY TO KILL ME IF YOU TURN NEGATIVE! THAT WILL BE THANKS ENOUGH!" That was the last human contact I had for more than a year.

I looked for stairs up the rock face. There wasn't any. Did the witch fly up there? On Limbo anything was possible. The island appeared to be as tall as it was broad. Steam wafted from the top of it. Great, I was on a volcano. Not only was I stranded, any day I might be consumed by a stream of lava.

I couldn't look up at the impossible task forever. I searched for handholds. They began to materialize, stretched a bit thin, but if I reached out far enough to my right or to my left, or above me, I just might make it to that ledge 50 meters up. After that I would reevaluate. Completing a series of smaller goals would eventually accomplish the larger task.

I got almost to the top of the ledge when something reacted negatively to me poking my hand into its burrow. It looked like a centipede, but it was as long as a small snake---at least 50 sims. I don't know if it was the painful bite, or the surprise. I lost my grip and fell onto the sand, barely missing several rocky protrusions. I couldn't move my legs. Was the paralysis caused by the insect or the severing of my spinal cord? It didn't matter. Neither scenario left me much hope.

I may have been hallucinating at the time, but I think I saw three or four giant crabs walking on their hind legs approach me. One grabbed my leg with its pincers. Was I going to lose consciousness before or after they ate me? All I knew was the eating was inevitable. They could have at least put me in a hot bath before consuming me. I would have done the same for them. It wasn't all bad. After I was re-created I would be able to walk again.

When I woke the grim reaper was standing over me, sans robe. I was on a wooden table in a room carved from stone. I was sore like I had been after my prior re-creations, but the overwhelming fatigue wasn't present. I tried to get up. My legs still wouldn't move.

"Did you come to my island to steal, to kill, or to satisfy your curiosity?" spoke an airy, crackly voice, indeterminate in age and gender. It sounded like the hinge of an old screen door.

I attempted to twist around, to see from whom--or what---the voice came. I knew who it had to be, but what would she look like? With my legs being dead the best I could do was expand my vision to my flanks. "I came to see you, to learn from you. Your name is Manta, isn't it?"

What came into view was no longer a woman. It looked like a seaweed covered piece of driftwood. She wore a muumuu. It appeared to be created from dried kelp. Her skin was weathered brown, stretched tight against her bones. Her hair was green, stringy, clustering strands that matted against her skull. Her irises were robin's egg blue. Her pupils were the darkest of blues, like what one would see far beneath the sea. "I'm not the grandmother you wish you had, am I? So, you shouldn't be heading to grandmother's house. Should I return you to the cru? They would have preferred to eat you, instead of bringing you to me. Perhaps I should cook you in my oven, and eat you myself."

"That might be for the best. When I'm re-created I won't be paralyzed any longer. Someone might as well get some use out of this broken body."

"You're a practical one, you are, but if I allow you to die you might be re-created far from here, and I do have a use for you. In exchange for you walking again I will require three years of your service. You have already offered to be my apprentice, but I have a greater need for an assistant, a go-fer, a gatherer for those things I can't gather. I will teach you what is necessary for you to know, but on a need-to-know basis. You may never learn everything you came here to learn. Do we have an agreement?"

If the witch could cure my paralysis, she ought to be able to teach me everything I wanted to know about the properties of elem and its management. Any collections I do will enhance my future business opportunities. "Agreed."

The thing I liked best about Manta, and there weren't many, was her directness. She didn't believe in idle chatter, or delaying when something needed to be done. No, I haven't always lived my life to that creed, but I did appreciate someone who did. I never had to second guess her. She did what she did for a purpose. Like a new recruit following the orders of a drill sergeant, I did everything asked of me. I knew Manta wouldn't waste my time playing games.

I visualized Manta being one of those wavy arm wizards

seen in cinemas. She was an herbalist. Elem was a byproduct of the terraforming process. Particles of energy are released from the planet. Different mediums release different particles. Green elem---elem terra---was released from the earth, the more fertile the denser the concentration. Blue elem---elem aqua---was from water, primarily found in seas. Yellow elem---elem aero---was found in the air, the higher the altitude, the fresher the air, the denser its concentration. Red elem---elem fiero---rises to the surface in hot areas, primarily in deserts, but also from volcanic vents. The Herb Islands had an exceptional concentration of elem, with elem fiero being the only variety found infrequently. It made sense now why Manta chose the island with the pseudo-dormant volcano as her home.

Collecting elem directly was complicated. Herbalists instead harvested particular plants that were most likely to contain elem within them. Manta had servants to do her bidding, but for her to sustain her control over them they had to remain on her island. Cru were too clumsy to safely collect anything, and her skeletal golem had difficulty completing complex tasks. Manta used elemites---small elementals---to collect her elem. They had a natural affinity for plants infused with elem. These clusters of earth, water, fire, and air roamed the island and its fringes, searching for appropriate vegetation. I never learned why the elemites did the witch's bidding, but I imagined it was kin to some form of companionship. Master and pet more likely than peers.

Each type of elem preformed a distinct function. Blue elem was used to heal. Green elem modified matter. Yellow elem modified movement. Red elem, was used to alter temperature, but also as a catalyst, when severe alterations were required.

I learned healing first---an extension of my paralysis being cured. A specific type of urchin was the most commonly collected source of blue elem in the Southern Sea. An animal's diet heavily influenced the type and probability of elem found within it. There were three primary categories of healing: disease, flesh, and energy. A spinal cord was one of the most complex areas to heal in a human body, but required just Flesh Healing. Less devastating injuries could require all three varieties of healing. A five elem cluster, called a penta, was required to release the energy. For Flesh Healing, four blue elem and one green were required. A pestle and mortar were used to grind four urchins with one mushroom. The powder was added to hot water, creating a broth. I was required to swallow the concoction. It made more sense to me to put it directly on the injury, but my body apparently assisted in its distribution, because within minutes I was able to move my legs.

"For three years from this moment, not a second less, I will retain your services."

I had my own room---and bed---thank Gaea. Manta never communicated with me except when she wanted something. Before I met Shell, I was used to living alone so the solitude didn't bother me. Manta's home consisted of catacombs within the semi-dormant volcano. Be it elem manipulation or servant toil, the construction was remarkable.

The day after I was healed, Manta put me to work. I spent the entire month collecting mushrooms. The task puzzled me, considering how much better the elemites were collecting them. I brought back the wrong kind the first day. My punishment was no food that evening, or the next morning. To ensure I had at least one suitable mushroom, I returned with samples of each variety found on the island. Manta frowned when she saw what I brought back, but one of them was the proper specimen, so she allowed me to eat. I got more proficient in collecting. Some days were better than others. I thought that with the goodwill I had accumulated, returning empty-handed one day wouldn't matter. Once again, I was deprived food. I learned to keep at least one harvested mushroom---of the proper variety---hidden away as a back-up. I never went hungry again.

The following month I was required to harvest the needles

of a certain evergreen found near the crest of the volcano. The secret was harvesting enough of them that some may contain elem, but not harvesting too much, killing the tree. The terrain was steep, so I was extremely cautious. I didn't want to break my back again and be in debt to the witch for another three years.

The third month involved harvesting lichen from the top of the volcano, just inside its rim. I definitely didn't want to fall into it. Sure, I would probably die and be re-created away from the island, but the death would be painful, and I still needed to learn more about the composition and management of elem.

My fourth month of service consisted of harvesting blue elem from urchins. This was my most difficult task. I couldn't breathe underwater, and Manta didn't provide me with any means to do so. There were rumored to be elem manipulations that permitted a man to breath underwater. Either Manta didn't know of these, or she believed there wasn't sufficient utility in consuming elem to collect elem. Fortunately, urchin lived in the shallows. Unfortunately, the island had few shallows---the beach I was dropped off on being the only one. I constructed a crude spear and with it I attempted to harpoon the spiny animals. The animals fought back. Like a porcupine, they defended themselves by releasing their quills. They weren't poisoned, but they stung as they entered me, and itched afterwards. I was least successful collecting these creatures. Manta must have realized how difficult the task was because she didn't deprive me of food when I returned empty-handed.

The remainder of the first year I harvested potential elem collectors haphazardly, one week collecting one variety of elem, the next, another. I rarely collected urchin. The elemites were much more efficient at it than I. Every day I brought something back to her, Manta would test it with that metal rod of hers. On average one time out of ten elem would be discovered. I did other things for her now, intermittently, like grinding elem-infused matter, and mixing it, but those occasions were rare.

At the beginning of my second year of servitude my service to Manta changed. "Now that you have become proficient in collecting elem-enriched specimens, you will begin the task I healed you for. The elem on this island are becoming depleted. I need you to collect some things for me on the mainland. There is the possibility that you may not return, but I must assume the risk. The need for you to complete your education will motivate you to fulfill your agreement. I have made preparations for your departure and return. Here are the things I require you to bring back to me."

All the specimens I was to harvest were in Chaneg, the Chaotic portion of the Negative Frontier. The transport elixir Manta provided had a limited range, but sufficient for me to reach the mainland. I was to transport approximately 50 kays to Hooter, the only settlement along the Chaotic-Neutral coast. To return to Curry Island I couldn't be much further away than that. The range of a transport penta was limited. Drowning would be preferable to the kays of swimming required if I came up short.

From Hooter I would travel due south, until I reached Simian Creek, which I would follow until I reached the Gibwoods.

Chapter 6

BAT

What would my relocation from Curry Island to Hooter consist of? After swallowing the elixir would I grow wings? Between blinks would I suddenly be in one place, then the other? It felt more like an out-of-body experience. I saw my surroundings change at an astonishing rate, but I didn't see myself. In the time it took me to respire I found myself on the outskirts of a cluster of three buildings. Across the street from them was a small dock that jutted into a calm sea.

Not seeing a road heading south, I walked into the hamlet to ask directions. A man was sitting on the porch of what looked to be a general store. The look he gave me was a cross between curiosity and loathing. "You're the first person that's come from Henriville today. The first solo in...weeks. Freight-haulers don't pass through here anymore. Boats sometimes stay for a spell, but they don't procrastinate. You're not planning on continuing east to Seaview? The Negative Frontier is just five kays away."

"I was planning on heading south. Where's the road that will take me that direction?"

The man nearly fell off his bench. "You sure you ain't no Infant? You don't look like one, but you're beginning to drool."

"I've got some business to do in the south. My business partner dropped me off here."

"Then one or both of you don't have much common sense. I never saw no boat arrive. Did you get dropped off down the coast? There are few places that a boat can moor."

"Something like that."

"If you're serious about heading south you need to go to Henriville first or Seaview. Both have roads heading south. Seaview is only 25 kays away, but it's in the Negative Frontier. I recommend going twice as far and having a safer journey."

"Thank you." I began walking towards Henriville. Then I thought about hiking those 25 kays in the wrong direction. Then I thought about meeting Shell, and having to explain that I wasn't ready to return to her. I darted into the jungle before I changed my mind again.

In the distance I heard, "Damn fool."

The jungle in Chanu didn't look any different than the one in Neutrality. It was humid, and dark, and there was a cacophony of superfluous animal sounds---as there were in Henryville. I was curious how Chaotic creatures would act differently than Neutral ones.

After travelling for an hour, I had my first atypical encounter. A brown bat with a meter wingspan began to follow me. I believed it to be just curious, but it continued to follow me. After a couple more kays of walking I became concerned. Was I its prey? Was it going to attack? If it was going to attack, why was it taking so long to do it?

The bat's movement changed. No longer was it flying overhead in long swoops, like it was taking a stroll. It appeared agitated. It flew in front of me, in a darting, swirling pattern, like a hummingbird might make. Was it going to attack, now? Was I giving off pheromones? Was it reacting to my emotions? The bat's movements became more intense. It was freaking out. Thoughts began to form in my mind. From my subconscious? Emotions. Images. Dusk. Gentle, warm breezes. Eating fruit. I began to feel more relaxed. The bat's intensity lessened. More fruit. I was having trouble staying awake. The bat landed on a branch beside me. The moss beneath the tree looked more comfortable than the wooden bed I slept on, on Curry Island. Just a five-minute nap, then I'll be able to make it the rest of the way out of the Weedwoods.

I awoke minutes...hours...days...later. It was still light, so it couldn't have been that long. The bat was resting on my stomach. Was it snoring? Its hide looked like it was made of black velvet. I stroked it. It twisted its head, then buried it into my shirt. This was the strangest pet I've ever had. Or maybe *I'm* the strangest pet it ever had. It looked so content. I didn't want to disturb it, not yet. Five minutes more. I still had a long way to go. I'll have to get up soon. It must have sensed my impatience, because it stirred, looked at me once, blinked, then flew off.

Using the stationary sun as my compass, I resumed my journey south. I didn't always see the bat, but whenever I became concerned it might have finally gotten tired of me, it would return, briefly, then dart back off. Sometimes it got agitated if I went a certain way, encouraging me to make a detour. Minutes later I would be given permission to return to my original course. The only rationale I had for this behavior was it knew danger was ahead and it wanted to keep it away from me.

At dusk I ate a few bites of dried fish, then slept in a place the bat had picked out for me: a hollowed-out log large enough for me to lie down in. I added leaves to the crumbly bark at its base. I slept soundly. I was confident if there was any danger the bat would notify me. I woke a couple of times in the middle of the night. Once, the bat was on me. The other, it wasn't. Bats were nocturnal. Night was its time to play.

When I woke---in the morning---the sun had already brightened. It had taken me more than a year to discover Limbo's sun never moved---it just changed its luminosity. The bat was back on me. I lay there for half an hour more. Sensing my impatience, again, the bat woke and flew off.

Midday, the jungle began getting less dense. A quarter later I saw open land ahead of me. The bat became agitated, but in a different manner. It became pleasantly excited. It swirled above me for a moment, then flew off.

I continued towards the plains. As I stepped out of the jungle I heard the bat approach. Someone was with it. "Not so much an infant anymore, Pulp Weedwood."

"Breeze?" The spotted felinoid strutted towards me in an elegant, at ease manner.

"But not grown up enough to know not to travel alone in the jungle. Did Az keep you company and out of trouble?" The bat consistently rubbed up against Breeze. In the manner and intensity it was carrying on I was amazed it remembered how to stay airborne.

"The company, was welcomed. The trouble, I believe I could have circumvented on my own alone. I've survived my share of hazards these past nine years."

Az flew in front of Breeze. It did a complex series of aerials. "Did you see the green widow's nest, or the elephant lizard, or the korren?"

"What's a korren?"

"A goat hybrid, about the size of a goat, but more amorous than a dog. It's not just your leg they'll rub."

"Did Az tell you all that?"

"In his way. He communicates at an emotional level and through a rudimentary sign language."

"Is he a demon?"

"No, he was never human. Gaea has blessed, and cursed, the feral nearly as often. Sometimes it's difficult to tell the two apart."

"I'm on my way to the Gibwoods."

"There are better routes to take."

"So I've been told."

"The further you go into a frontier the more likely you'll meet extreme examples of its morality. There are things more Chaotic than the korren."

"There is something I need to do in the Gibwoods."

"This is something Manta put you up to, isn't it? You've become her apprentice?"

"I've only learned to extract specimens for her so far. Before she will teach me more I must collect a few things in the Gibwoods."

"The witch hasn't been known to leave her island, at least in the decades I've been alive."

"Are you really...."

"I've been on Limbo at least as long as she has. I lost count after my third decade. Some of us become bored. They are the ones who become arboreals or elementals. Others try to re-event themselves. Sometimes Gaea does it for us. Those of us who live in Chaos are very creative in the manner we entertain ourselves. I like to help people, but not always in the manner they desire. You look much more fit."

"Limbo does that to you. You either get more fit or more exotic."

"I'm willing to play with you in a more intimate manner, but I must warn you I'm not ordered enough to retain a relationship." Before I could formulate a response, she added, "No, I've changed my mind. I no longer wish to become intimate with you. You seem too much like a brother to me."

"Thanks."

"I mean that in a good way. You are the baby brother I helped raise. The one who names often forms a kinship to the one that is named. That's why I sent Az to find, then look after you."

Saying she was like a sister, didn't make her one. I imagined what it would be like to be intimate with her, someone sexy who wasn't quite human. I came to love Shell in a familiar way, but Breeze was special. And I think she always will be. She was in a different league than Shell. She was a celebrity you had a crush on, but knew you had no hope of having a relationship with. Why was I thinking such thoughts? Was the contrast of being with the witch for a year to re-discovering Breeze too much for me? Was being in the Chaotic Frontier making me crazy? I needed to leave Breeze's prescience as soon as possible.

"I need to be going. I enjoyed our re-acquaintance, and appreciate Az looking out for me, but the sooner I complete my task for Manta the sooner I can leave her employment."

"You can't get rid of me that easily. Az and I are coming with you. The Gibwoods are no place for a youngster to be traveling alone. And who knows, maybe I'll forget you're my brother some time during our journey."

Great. I probably needed the help, but I didn't need the distraction, and Breeze was definitely going to distract me.

"The Burlap Plains are where a majority of cotton is grown on Limbo. Most of the crop is funneled through Saint Charles. It's 30 kays to the west, so we won't be passing through it. The Burlap

Plains also has fire toads, dust elementals, 20-meter long snakes, and kreen. Kreen are insects the size of a horse, and at least as fast. They are nomads. They have been known to hunt anything that moves. Sometimes for food, but often just for sport. If we see them, it is too late. Clouds of dust on the horizon, we'll bypass. It might just be an elemental, but they're not all that pleasant either. There are some places abrasive grit doesn't need to go. We'll sleep in the jungle the remainder of the day, and travel after sundim. The kreen aren't nocturnal, but Az is, giving him good night vision. He'll be able to warn us of any danger."

When I woke in the middle of night to urinate I noticed Az tucked between Breeze's breasts. The next few days will be torture.

Chapter 7

SHOES

The moon was bright enough for us to see nearly as far as in daylight, which, in a prairie, was substantial. Az would periodically leave us, but with the land being so open we never completely lost sight of him. I hadn't seen any cotton yet. Crops were a novelty to me. When I was bulkier it took too much effort to drive into the country.

Well into the second hour of our midnight stroll, the grass disappeared, not completely, but instead of it being knee high it was closer to a sim. "This might make is easier to walk, but potentially more dangerous," Breeze informed me. "Mowers---

locust the size of mice---eat everything in their path. Every three years a swarm forms large enough to wipe out this entire prairie."

We accelerated our pace. Az frantically returned to us. Breeze translated. "A band of kreen are heading our way. Mowers have caused a nocturnal evacuation." The telltale curtain of dust was prominent in the direction Az had come from. Breeze altered our course to due east. She dropped to all fours. I had to push myself to keep up with her. Trees were just ahead of us. Could we have walked far enough already for them to be the Gibwoods?

About the time the river came into view I remembered the Gibwoods were south and we had turned east. This must be Simian Creek, the stream Manta suggested I follow. Breeze turned around. "If the kreen come much closer we must cross the creek. Something they won't do unless they come to a ford---they can't swim. We'll follow along the bank the remainder of the night."

I know I should have been watching where I was going---I tripped half-a-dozen times---but I couldn't keep my eyes off what could be coming towards us from the prairie. "Should we cross now?"

"No."

"Now?"

"No." Breeze was trying to be patient with me, but I was beginning to get on her nerves, so I toned it down.

Something flashed. A minute later, another flash, followed by a flaming plume. Smoke continued to billow after the bright light had ceased. It took a moment for the outline of the flames to fade from where it had burned into my retinas. Breeze giggled. "Apparently more than kreen have been displaced this evening."

"I'm pleased one of us finds humor in the situation. Weren't the kreen once human? Do you really wish them to be burned alive?"

"The life they led was the catalyst for the form they now find themselves in. A consequence of that lifestyle is being burned alive."

"It could have easily been us."

"But it wasn't. We chose to head towards the creek. Gaea permits self will."

We didn't have to cross the creek. I was mildly disappointed. What would Breeze look like dog...ah...cat-paddling? The Gibwoods were reached a quarter before moon-brighten. The temperate deciduous forest, with its delicate, opaque-leaved, broad branched trees were a welcomed change. All I had seen the past eight years were palms, conifers, and a few waxy leaved trees. We continued to parallel the river until we came to a copse of ancient oaks.

Initially, I believed Leech had intended to stop here because of the beauty of the large, droopy branches, but after seeing a swarm of mosquitoes, very large ones, I wasn't so certain. The moon began to brighten as one of the mosquitoes came up to me. I was about to slap it, then I noticed it wasn't really an insect. It was a small person, less than 10 sims from head to toe. I couldn't tell if it was a man or a woman. It had gossamer wings, but also clothes. They were of bright colors: reds, yellows, and oranges. They looked like they were weaved from autumn leaves. The one hovering in front of me looked like a butterfly---wearing shoes. Shoes? Fashion often superseded practicality.

The creatures were curious of me, but Breeze was their focus. Dozens of them buzzed around her like she was a meadow of wildflowers. Az wasn't left out. The bat was not only mobbed, but landed upon, like he was an aircraft carrier.

After many more minutes of adoration Breeze introduced me. "There are many tribes of faerie on Limbo, but this is my favorite." The faerie's buzzing was non-stop. "No...no...wait...until I finish speaking with the unchanged."

"Can you understand that buzzing?"

"It's not really buzzing. If you listen carefully, it's Esperanto, but higher pitched, and the words spoken more rapidly. Slow down if you also wish the human to hear your tales. They have phenomenal imaginations. They spend most of the day creating stories. Nearly all their waking hours. Sometimes also in their dreams. When they wake they immediately tell someone before they forget. If you concentrate you may be able to understand them. If not, their voices are still pleasing to the ear. You don't have to understand what they are saying to be moved by it. I sleep best falling asleep to one of their serenades. Which reminds me, it's time for a nap."

Breeze lay down beneath one of the grand old oaks. She curled up in a ball on the bright green grass. I attempted to understand what the faerie were saying, but caught just a word or two. I couldn't find any clarity in connecting the intermittent thoughts together. After a few minutes I could barely keep my eyes open. Being stubborn, I tried not to fall asleep. I eventually lost the battle, much sooner than I thought possible.

Chapter 8

HEART

One of the best methods of gauging what time it was, was by the temperature. The sun never moved, and I haven't yet seen a clock. One must use the tools they are given. Temperature wasn't a precise method, but one could determine if it was early or late morning, noon, or early or late afternoon. When I woke it was about noon.

The faerie offered Breeze and me a thimble-sized serving of nectar. To them it would have appeared to be a barrel. I politely declined, not wishing to deprive them of such a substantial quantity, but Leech insisted, informing me it would be rude to refuse. It was delicious, very sweet, but strong. The nectar must have spent many weeks fermenting. It was more a schnapps than juice.

We left shortly after drinking our faerie tea. The faerie had separation anxiety. They followed us for nearly a kay. When we came to a bridge---a clear sign of civilization---they finally returned to their copse.

A road followed the creek the remainder of the way to St. Francis, the only human settlement in the Gibwoods. “I believe I can make it the rest of the way,” I told Breeze. “I know how you feel about cities.”

“What you’re collecting is unlikely to be in the city.”

“Manta said it was just south. It grows along the bluff overlooking the river.”

“What’s it called?”

“Knowing the name wouldn’t mean anything to me, so she didn’t name it. That’s her way. She did describe it. I’ll know it when I see it.”

“My disdain for cities hasn’t changed. I never go into Henriville, and St. Francis has twice as many people. I’ll circle around the village and meet you tomorrow on the bluff. Before you get all noble on me and suggest you will also bypass the city, I perceive your desire to spend a night in a bed, as strong as mine to sleep in a faerie copse. Enjoy your bed and your hot bath. Maybe on the way back to the coast, if you wish to wash again, I can do it for you.” I couldn’t tell if she was sincere. I contemplated the activity and was both abhorred and aroused.

St. Francis was a lumber town. In a world without combustion engines, or many beasts of burden, it would take some work to haul the lumber out of the Gibwoods. The creek must have been used, but I hadn’t yet seen a barge. All the buildings in Gibb were constructed of wood, even the centrally located five-story

Wood Exchange. I slept in the *Inn At The End*, a modest two-story structure. The ten rooms above the pub were half full.

I splurged on a hot bath, the first since I've been a resident of Limbo. Shell and I swam in the sea when we were dirty. I did the same on Curry Island. I don't believe Manta ever bathed. Somehow, she never stank. Like the rest of the world, dirt didn't want anything to do with her. I spent the first five minutes washing, then I just soaked. I must have fallen asleep, because I woke when someone began pounding on the bathroom door. The water had cooled to room temperature. I was shivering. After putting on my dirty clothes---I hadn't noticed how bad they smelled while I was as dirty as they were---I opened the door. The innkeeper's assistant gave me a dirty look, then proceeded to drain the water.

I went downstairs and ate until I ran out of money.

I cautiously climbed into bed. I didn't see any of the bugs old world inns were infamous for, but most were supposedly microscopic.

I awoke refreshed. I wasn't itching, so I may have dodged the lice, bed bugs and scabies. The moon was just beginning to brighten, but I didn't wish to wait any longer---I was almost done with my task. I ate a piece of dried fish, packed my small pack, walked downstairs, then out the door.

By the time I reached the bluff south of the city, it was completely light. I was more cautious than I would have been before overhearing a very disturbing conversation in the pub.

"Where's Cyprus?"

"He was killed yesterday."

"FEEK! That's three this month."

"Gib?"

"No feek, ogre-borer."

"Gaea. What happened to the good old days, when a tree falling the wrong direction took someone out, or an axe or saw dismembered them?"

"And it's getting worse. For some Gaea awful reason, the people killed by gib are being re-created as gib. The population is booming."

"Maybe you're boring them and they're having babies."

I had to interrupt. "What do these gib look like?" I couldn't complete my mission if I was dead. And I definitely didn't want to be mutated into one of these things. My service to Manta was temporary. What a way to spend the rest of my life. Attacking, and presumably eating, other people? Of course, they wouldn't look like people to me anymore. What would they taste like? Chicken? Or Steak?

"Kind of like a gorilla. Short black hair, except for on their heads, where its bushier."

"But their faces are more like a chimpanzee's. Pink. Like their ears. Which are more elongated. Like a mule's."

"They carry sharpened sticks."

"Which they will either throw at you. Or stab you."

"Once they draw blood, their instincts take over. They'll rip out your throat with their teeth, then untangle your intestines."

"Have you tried to eradicate them?" I asked them.

"By doing what? Calling an exterminator?"

"They haven't been that much of a problem until recently, when their population began to swell. There's easier prey deeper in the woods."

"A group last year made an attempt. It only added to the problem."

"Everyone killed?"

"More died than came back to tell the tale."

The plant I was looking for was three meters tall. Its leaves resembled an olive tree's. Its central column was broad. Atop it were golden tendrils, resembling corn silk. The plant was supposedly one of the few specimens that always had elem in it. I didn't have to harvest the entire plant. The elem resided in its heart, a rosy nodule a third of a way down from its tendrils.

The first plant I located that met the description Manta gave me looked dead. The heart looked like it had been cut out. Sap had dripped from the wound and hardened. The plant was withered, and bent forward. The next four plants I saw were in a similar state.

Two kays from the first plant, I finally found one that was healthy. I reached up with the dagger Shell had given me on our first anniversary. On a planet as harsh as Limbo what better gift to give someone? The breeze must have picked up, because the plant began to shake. The flesh of the plant was surprisingly soft. I was careful to leave the heart completely intact. As I pulled the rose nodule towards me the plant convulsed. Sap leaked out, first as a healthy torrent, then as a drizzle.

As I placed the fist-sized heart into my collection bag, Breeze ran up to me, her hind legs passing her forelegs, then falling back again. She nearly knocked me over. "WHAT ARE YOU DOING?!"

"I'm collecting the specimens I told you about."

"You never mentioned you were going to do this. The plant is...was...alive. It was once human."

I couldn't restrain the revulsion I felt. I bent over, then vomited, some of it landing on my boots.

Breeze's expression was frozen in shock. Az flew madly, one moment high in the sky, the next, diving towards the earth.

I withdrew the heart from the bag and attempted to replace it in the cavity I created. It stayed there, for a minute, then it fell to the ground with a thud. The plant had already lost its turgidity. It slumped forward, half looking at its heart, half at me.

The commotion was a beacon for the gib. They subsisted on chaos and I provided plenty of it. My last thought was for Breeze's safety. Was she able to escape? I'm certain Az did, unless the bat made itself vulnerable in order to save its companion. I didn't care about myself. I didn't even fight them off.

Chapter 9

TREES

I woke in a place I had never been before. The trees were all conifers, and much taller than any I've experienced so far in Limbo. What mutations would manifest this time? I looked down at my body, then felt my head. The distress wasn't because I lost too much of my humanity. I hadn't lost enough. I killed someone. Worse than killing them, because the act not only ended their life, it may have cursed them to spend the next in a much less desirable state and location.

My body had become hairless and elongated. My ears were now pointed, like a devil's. My bulk diminished again. I was actually on the skinny side now. Becoming more aware of my surroundings, in relation to my size, I realized it wasn't that. I hadn't lost weight, I had gained height. I was more than a meter taller than I had been before the gib mangled me. I had become a giant, but not a fierce, hairy, brutal beast. I had become nearly feminine in my smoothness.

Where was I? Hell was fitting for the crime I had committed. But this place didn't look like hell. Not the version I was raised to fear. If my true morality was the complete opposite of who I thought I was, did that mean I was the type of person who did things for the wrong reasons, inconsistently? Was I in Chaneg, the Chaotically-Negative Frontier? What other creatures might I meet here? Would they be as despicable as I? Or more so?

I chose to live a solitary life, partially because I was afraid of what I might meet, but more so because I was embarrassed to expose myself to public scrutiny. To punish myself, I chose not to build a shelter. I slept under the stars---moon actually. Either the moon washed out the night sky or I was on an artificial world. I lay on leaves and moss. Sometimes, even bare ground. During the day I ruminated about what I had done. One day I would make up for it, somehow. I just couldn't come up with a penitence great enough---yet. I ate what I could find. Nuts. Berries. Roots. Sometimes even wild onions or sweet grass.

I chose not to hunt. I killed too many already. Not just the watchwood, as I later learned it was called, but scores of others through less direct actions.

What did the watchwood watch? The canyon below, and the river that flowed through it? Was there a limit in how far they could see? All the way to the horizon, where the curvature of the planet made the land disappear? Did their observations consist of more than seeing? Did they also perceive? Analyze? Investigate? Evaluate? Scrutinize?

Did I do it a favor? Living years as a tree had to be boring. No, I couldn't rationalize my guilt away like that.

Even if I wanted to hunt, I wouldn't be able to eat the meat. I no longer had incisors. I had only molars, like a horse, and they were nearly as large. I could grind food efficiently, but I couldn't tear it. I was a giant, but one that couldn't eat meat. What fun was that?

Early into my second year as a giant a wolf began to follow me. At night it would curl up beside me. I would play with it during the day. I began feeling guilty, that I didn't deserve someone so loyal. If it knew what I had done it wouldn't want to be my companion any longer. I shooed it away, first by telling it to go, then by throwing things at it. It got the idea after an hour of me mistreating it.

To relieve my boredom, I made a game out of seeing how often I could hit a trunk with a stone or a stick. I became quite proficient. My eyesight and hand-eye coordination were much improved in this form. The only problem I had was the limited range of the materials I used. I made myself a bow---and arrows. Constructing the bow was relatively easy. Making an arrow that flew straight, wasn't. Through trial and error, over many weeks, I had constructed a dozen arrows that were able to hit their mark a majority of the time.

The novelty of archery eventually wore off. I began to explore outside the few hundred hectares I called my home. I hadn't yet encountered another person since my re-creation in Chaneg. Was I the only one here? Was my crime so heinous I had to be isolated?

I believed they were monkeys, initially. They behaved in a frivolous manner, but joyously. There was a lot of chasing and tackling---and fornicating. I walked away, embarrassed my reconnaissance had morphed into voyeurism. This was definitely not what I should be doing seeking penitence.

The creatures looked more human the longer I studied them. Their naked bodies were lank and hairy. Their limbs were elongated. The genders were tempered, but distinct. They lived in the forest canopy. Ladders and swinging bridges led to gazebos and cottages.

Arbols? So, maybe I wasn't re-created in the Negative Frontier. What mixed-up world would reward someone for being a murderer?

A few days later my questions were answered. When I woke one morning I found the forest had suddenly closed in upon me. The trees that surrounded me varied in height from four to six meters. They were of different species. If one placed the watchwood at one end of a spectrum and humans at the other end, they would be in the middle. Branches moved as arms, and roots as legs. Each had a knot in its trunk that was a caricature of a countenance.

"The arbols asked us to welcome you to the neighborhood."

Wind swirled through branches, rustling leaves as the eddies ebbed and flowed. Sounds combined to form words.

"I didn't think the arbols knew I was there."

"They knew. They just didn't care." The tone was slightly different, so it must have come from another tree.

"They didn't care for themselves," a third spoke.

"They were concerned for you," spoke a forth, or was it the first or second again?

"You appeared lost." I perceived it wasn't speaking solely of my location.

Sometimes one of them began before the prior had finished. It was difficult for me to keep up, for me to keep one thought isolated from another. At times the swirling winds became a storm.

"You have questions."

"We have seen much."

"Have lived much."

"Primaries."

"Original inhabitants."

"Communication."

"Across Limbo."

"Through the winds."

"Through the earth."

"More reliable."

"But slower."

There was no longer any doubt I was in the Chaotic Frontier. I slowly felt my sanity fading. My residual orderliness required affirmation. "So, I'm in Chapo?"

"Yes."

"How could I be if I committed murder prior to dying and being re-created?"

"Mind."

"Not acts."

"So, in my mind I had become more Positive?"

"After the act the mind changed."

"I don't deserve to be here."

"Your mind says you do."

"Your soul says you do."

"We retain our soul when we are re-created?"

"Only our soul."

"Matter is filler."

"So, killing the watchwood wasn't that heinous?"

"The soul determines."

"You were an instrument in its modification."

"Not architect."

"Gaea."

"Producer."

"Not director."

"Not creator."

"So, I could have returned with the watchwood hearts?"

"Always consequences."

"Soul within the watchwood heart."

"Near the elem?"

"Soul is the elem."

"If I had given Manta the watchwood hearts, what would she have done with them?"

"Slaves."

"Golems."

"Golems have souls?"

"Some golems."

"Sovereign golems."

"Semi-sovereign golems."

"The skeletal golem didn't seem to be very intelligent, but the....were the elemites enslaved souls?"

"Elements have been used to board soul slaves."

"I should have gone to hell."

"Morally modified."

"Gaea determines."

"Self determines."

"What am I to do now? How can I make reprimands?"

"As you see fit."

"Infinite options."

"What profession shall I choose? Does Limbo need a hairless, pointed-eared giant?"

There was a brief interlude of branches rubbing and leaves and needles shaking. I sensed I was being laughed at.

"Go to others of your kind."

"Other hairless, pointed eared giants?"

Another interlude of rubbing and shaking.

"Each unique."

"Seek Toe."

"Western Sea."

The cacophony of sonic swirling gave me a headache. I messaged my temples. More laughter. "Do you find my appearance humorous? Is it my head? My skin? Your bark is also bald." Louder laughter.

They left me, barely able to walk on their roots. Their shaking left a pile of leaves and needles behind.

Was Toe the name of someone who lived near the Western Sea? Beside it? In it? Where was this sea? I could ask the arbols. No, I couldn't, not with them thinking I was a peeping tom. It might be years before I could look them in the eye. I headed west.

Chapter 10

GENTS

Sixty kays I walked, the first 20 in the wrong direction. It was reasonable for the Western Sea to be in the west, but the west of Limbo, not necessarily west of me. I was already about as far west as one could be and still be within the force barrier that ensconced the penal colony.

The barrier was an indefinitely high wall that protected the planet from the inmates. Why didn't the wardens use the entire planet? There were conjectures. We would annihilate one another more efficiently if we were closer together. Limbo wasn't the only penal colony on the planet. Or, most likely, we were contained in a smaller space to minimize resources.

The energy screen was opaque. I could almost distinguish shapes beyond it. Outlines. Shadows. Fearful of electrocution, I was content to examine it from afar.

I arrived at the Western Sea at sundim---of the second day. The moon shining on the ocean created a beautiful setting. A harbinger of what my life would be like once I met this Toe?

I watched the moon reflecting off the water for an hour. Not wishing this moment to end, I intended to extend it as long as possible. Nothing bothered me. I was too far from the water to be the prey of those who inhabited the sea, and too close to those who inhabited the land. I observed a herd of sea horse swim by shortly after my arrival. The aquamarine equines were five meters long, from elongated head to tail fin. Plains were often compared to oceans. For these creatures, the opposite was true.

I contemplated capturing one, to tame it as a steed. Before I conceived of a means to do so, I remembered the Human Pact. Being no longer human, it no longer applied to me, technically, but that didn't diminish its benefit---like people banding together for mutual protection. Its corollary, that we shouldn't enslave animals because they could have once been human, was more complicated. Could have didn't mean were. Human freight-haulers were inefficient beasts of burden. Demon-freight was more efficient, but less reliable.

Shortly after the moon brightened, after sleeping an hour-and-a-half propped against a sea oat speckled sand dune, a large bird flew towards me. I first noticed it high in the sky. It glided to the ground. It grew in size as it came closer. The seagull became an eagle, then a pterodactyl. The size of one. It looked like a golden eagle. There was something on its back: a golden-skinned man wearing a golden robe. He had a long beard, also golden, that danced wildly in the aerial breeze. He was much smaller than the bird: half its body, a fourth of its wingspan.

When the bird finally landed a few meters in front of me I was knocked off my feet. The molecules it displaced had to go somewhere.

The man dismounted. He walked towards me, towering over me, as tall as a two-story building. He lowered his hand down to me. I clutched it. It was nearly three times the size of mine, and as firm as rubber. He pulled me up, lifting my 200 kilos as effortlessly as a piece of balsa wood. He set me back down. He appraised me with eyes that had seen more than I would see in several lifetimes. They smiled. "Welcome to the Brotherhood." His voice boomed, shaking the sand, and causing ripples in the shallows of the sea.

I stared up at him. Manta was an invalid compared to the creature before me. His prescience alone demanded respect. He was the parent, and I, the small child. He the leader, I, the follower. No question. No uncertainty.

"I am Toe Serpent Glade. My companion is Olive."

"I am Pulp Weedwood. Your name was mentioned as one I should contact."

"As you should have, years ago, when you were first rewarded this form."

"I've been busy, and have just recently learned of you."

"You've been busy watching the arbols." My face reddened. Toe's eyes laughed. "Nothing wrong with a young man becoming curious. Being creatures of chaos, we permit ourselves to be mischievous. Those up north wouldn't approve, or understand. It's best you not mention it to them."

My neck was getting sore from looking up. I backed up a couple of strides. "Toe?"

"I was named many years before I became a gent. I died by stubbing my toe. Feek happens. The trail of blood my foot made led the piranhas to me."

"Gent? That sounds like you'll rather be thought of as a gentleman than a brute."

"To my Positive brethren, the term does request a certain amount of dignity. To my Negative, it demands respect. Lord or Lady this or that ruling his or her lands with an iron fist."

"Will I get to ride on Olive?"

"If she allows. If her mood sours, the journey isn't entirely without merit. We have made introductions. And I can still inform you of the politics of the Brotherhood."

"The Brotherhood?"

"The Brotherhood of Giants was created 24 years ago to counter the power of the Wizards. And to a lesser extent, draks. Drak are stronger than gents, individually, but not collectively. We meet at least once a year to discuss issues, and to determine if we need to pool our power to make a political statement. Of late there are those who also wish to make social statements, but fortunately they are in a minority."

"How many...gents...are there in the Brotherhood?"

"You will be the sixteenth. We of the Positive Faction welcome you with open arms. Those of the Negative won't be as appreciative of your re-creation. You see, before your arrival the Brotherhood had 3 Positive gents, 6 Neutrals, and 6 Negatives. When at least five of the Neutrals choose to vote with us, as they often do, we have a majority. All the Negative Faction needs to do to get one of their proposals passed is to sway two Neutral votes, which occasionally happens. With an additional Positive, it will require three."

"When will the Brotherhood next meet?"

"As soon as you are willing. Before, if your hesitancy lingers. A meeting is mandatory whenever a new member joins the Brotherhood, to introduce, and christen."

"I'm going to be submersed?"

"You're confusing a christening with a baptism. Christening will consist of you pledging yourself to the Brotherhood in the prescience of your peers. All must be present for this to occur, for you to become a member of the Brotherhood. Many years ago, a gent boycotted the christening, to deny the new member. As punishment, he was ostracized, removing him---and his vote---from the Brotherhood. He begged to be permitted to return. After a year of penance, consisting of him assisting other gents in anything they desired, he was allowed to return. The new gent, promptly christened, assigned many strenuous and unsanitary jobs to his antagonist."

The flight on Olive was harrowing---yes, she graciously permitted me to ride her. My appreciation was expressed as scraps of food thrown her way whenever I could, continuing many years past our initial introduction. They didn't amount to much, relative to her size, but I believe she appreciated the attention. Toe lived on a cloud island above the Crosshairs---where Limbo's four seas met. How it was able to support the weight of a mansion was beyond me. The surface of the cloud felt like sponge rubber. I bounced a bit as I walked on it. I fell a couple of times, but eventually got used to it. The most important thing Toe taught me was what I might expect from each gent. Everyone had his or her own agenda, as unique and encompassing as personality. For many, the two were interchangeable.

"I was told the moral extremes were quarantined to the Frontier."

"We are compelled to remain. Short excursions are mild irritants."

"This doesn't look like a vacation home."

"Sacrifices must be made to ensure the survival of the Brotherhood. I return to the Positive Frontier periodically. Departing is uncomfortable, but not debilitating. You'll be safe at Cloud Home. Not so if you choose to leave it before you have been christened. A gent may not harm another gent, but before you are christened you are just a tall demon. That is why I said you should have contacted me sooner than you did. Someone from the Negative Faction may have killed you before you were christened. It has happened before. And it usually takes more than one death to mutate out of being a gent. Being sought, and killed, repeatedly, after re-creation isn't a pleasant existence."

"But I just recently learned of you?"

"Isolation doesn't free one from trouble or obligation."

Toe's brothers, and sisters, arrived via portal, a necessity due to their dispersal. No, the portal couldn't be modified to free me. The portals the gents employed weren't strong enough to breach the energy shield that confined us.

The gents gathered in the center of the cloud cluster, around an immense circular table: two meters high to accommodate their height, ten meters across to accommodate their bulk. Servants served food from its hollow center. Being half the size of a human, the gnobs, as they were called, easily walked beneath the table without stooping. They had volunteered to assist the gents in exchange for an emigration from their dreary subterranean dwellings. A temporary relocation, Cloud Home's staff rotated, simultaneously alleviating home sickness and wanderlust.

I was tremendously apprehensive meeting my peers. It felt like the first day of school, without any of the excitement that accompanied the dread. I didn't really think of them as my peers, more like people I was forced to associate with.

The better-behaved brethren were first to arrive. Urchin lived on an atoll in the Western Sea. He was half again as tall as I. He wore just a loin cloth. When one was a gent, he could wear whatever he wished. "So, you must be Pulp," he spoke in a deep, but gentle voice, like waves crashing against the shore. Something the size of a gent couldn't make a completely quiet sound. "I'm just up the coast from you. Come by if you need anything."

"Thank you."

I turned to Toe and whispered, "How far away is Urchin, from where I live?"

"Two-hundred kays."

"Two-hundred kays? I guess I won't be borrowing sugar from him."

"Two-hundred kays isn't as far to someone our size as it is to the unchanged." That's true. "But why walk when you can fly or use a portal?"

"I can have a portal?"

"All gents receive a portal---after they're christened. How effective would our coalition be without the ability to concentrate and disperse our power?"

The other Positive gent, Fir, wasn't exactly unfriendly, but he wasn't as outgoing as Urchin. He had a more serious demeanor. He had a professional athlete's build and great posture. He was just a couple of sims taller than I, but appeared taller. He wore a leather jerkin and shorts. He had a beard, but it was neatly trimmed. He lived in the Platinum Mountains, in Orpo. "Good day." His greeting was excessively cordial. A hint of resentment stuck to the syrup. My arrival may assist his causes, but it also brought change. Orderly individuals didn't like change.

"I'm looking forward for this day to end," I said.

"Indeed. Existence is a necessary evil."

The other gents began to filter in, first appearing every five minutes, then one after another. They varied in size from my height to Toe's. In a group with so much Negativity, the leader was obligated to be the biggest and strongest. Some of the gents wore practically nothing. Others many layers, notably, armor. Many of the gents ignored me, while others challenged me with dreadful stares. I stayed close to the ones I believed wouldn't harm me.

We sat in a particular order around the table, determined by our morals. I sat between Toe and Urchin. To the left of Urchin were two Chaotically-Neutral gents. Boulder lived in the Honey Mountains in the south. He looked like a cave man, wearing a leather loincloth and boots and carrying a club. Beside him was a two-headed gent: Toad & Stool. One of his heads was pleasant. The other, less so. To his/their left were three Chaotic Negative gents. Lord Bruin, as he called himself, looked like Boulder, but he was two meters taller and carried a large battle axe. He wore armor on his chest and head. Two large horns stuck out of the latter. Lord Dung's most notable feature was his single eye. No, he wasn't a cyclops. There was evidence of a second eye: an injury that didn't heal. Gaea usually wasn't so untidy, but there were as many cursed by her as were blessed. He also wore the hide loincloth and boots that were prevalent with the Negative gents. Lord Thump was the arch-typical gent. He wore a hide that hung from one shoulder. He carried a prickly wooden club and wore no shoes. All three lived in the Dreadful Mountains, in the heart of the Moral Bulge. The next two gents lived in the Neutral-Negative Frontier. Lady Palm, in the Sabre Desert. She wore a beige robe and scarf that covered her flawlessly, with the exception of her eyes and hands. Lord Nettle, in the Grim Mountains. Something must have gone wrong when he was re-created. One arm was too long. The other too short. He had a hump on his back, and blemishes on his skin. His hair, on his head and body, grew in patches. Lord Coal was the lone Negative-Order gent. He was a dark-skinned redhead who wore bronze armor. He lived in Pyramid Sands. The first Neutral was Granite. He lived in the Northern Spine Mountains. He was as bald as I, but twice as tall. Scree was the second tallest gent after Toe. He lived in the Southern Spine, near Gulag. He wore a robe that draped from one shoulder. He was the most sophisticated of the group. A task not too difficult to achieve. He was also the gent who socialized with humans the most often, due to his proximity to their pseudo-capital. The last Neutral was Jasmine. She lived in a jungle in the Liver Peninsula. She wore a bikini that barely contained her bounty. She was the antithesis of Lady Palm. Mist was the loan Neutral-Order gent. He lived on an island in the Northern Sea. He also wore a loincloth. His albino skin and hair blended in well with his frequently foggy environment. And finally, there was Fir, who sat beside Urchin.

After introductions were given, I was required to stand in the center of the table and give my allegiance to the Brotherhood.

"Pulp Weedwood, I welcome you into the Brotherhood of Giants. With our unity may we never be subjected to the whims of others."

"SO HELP US GAEA!" my peers roared. When giants did anything in unison the earth shook. I regained my hearing many minutes later.

We ate a wonderful feast. As was tradition, the gents brought something from their native lands. A gent's potluck was a feast for not only the stomach and eyes, but also the nose. The mixed odors were too much for me at times. It would have been an unpleasant experience for someone to be directly below the cloud island when I returned some of the food over its edge.

Politics were discussed, but our focus was on the food. Waste products were thrown as far as a gent could throw them. For someone who could throw a boulder with ease, that was considerable. *Giant's Rain* kept the sea creatures below well fed for days.

"There are now penta shops in every city, and nearly every town," stated Granite. "It's a sign of things to come. Having footholds will make it easier for the Wizards to rule."

"Which won't happen if we destroy the penta shops," Lord Nettle suggested.

"Which will bring their wrath upon us," stated Fir.

"So be it," said Lord Coal. "This war will be upon us some day. Why not begin it at a time of *our* choosing?"

"How do we know that attacking them now isn't a time of *their* choosing?" Fir suggested. "Neither expansion or reconnaissance, but bait."

The discussion, and many others, persisted throughout the day. There was talk of imbibing intoxicating substances, but that was one of two things Toe didn't tolerate at Cloud Home---the other being violence. It was unsafe to be impaired thousands of meters above the earth.

Some of the gents pulled me aside to discuss issues in private. If I supported them with *this,* they might support me later with *that*. Being a novice, they assumed my naiveté would put me at a disadvantage. I made no promises, but seeds of their beliefs had sprouted in my mind.

Chapter 11

BOREDOM

I remained with Toe for a few more days, then returned to the Copper Forest. I intended to build myself a mansion, like the majority of my brothers, but never got around to it. The entire forest was my home. I slept when I got tired, on needles, in a cave.... It didn't matter, as long as no one bothered me. Most were wise enough not to do so.

I felt it finally time to contact the arbols. Me watching them in the past was a non-issue to them. Being taller and stronger, I was able to provide substantial assistance, the majority of it, unsolicited. Some of their women were fascinated with me in other ways. It had been nearly three years since I've been with Shell. After many weeks of begging, I gave in to their experimentation. I was apprehensive at first: my rustiness being as much an issue as the difference in our sizes. Everything worked out---quite well, actually. The demand being much greater than the supply, I never lacked physical intimacy when I wished it. Emotional intimacy was another issue. Being chaotic creatures, arbols were, how I should put it?---flaky. They lived for the moment. Their collective shallow thoughts occasionally added up to a deep one. Not often enough for me.

I began to get bored. A wide palette of mythical stimuli and I get bored. It's been said that being bored is a state of mind. There are no boring situations, just boring people, so mentally---and emotionally---lazy they wait for the world to entertain them rather than entertain themselves. When Toe suggested I join a group of adventurers traveling the world, I jumped at the opportunity.

Adventure wasn't the only thing they were seeking. There was a great treasure. Not gold, gems, or jewels. They sought a means to free themselves from Limbo. An evacuation portal was discovered, but in pieces, widely scattered. The first was found shortly before I joined the group. The second, shortly after. Over many weeks, and many changes in our composition, we collected two more pieces. Four spheres now, out of six, electromagnetically joined.

Our current permutation consisted of Hornet, Stick, Centaur, Cone---all humans. General Paint---a trog. And myself. We had just extricated the Amber Sphere from a *lich*, a partially-dead elem wielder. We tended to our injuries as we camped in an abandoned subterranean-arbol city. Large mushrooms towered above us. Windows, doors, entire rooms, were carved out of the artificial fungi that rose five stories, all empty now. A glowing orb---a diminutive replica of the artificial sun illuminating the surface---illuminated the cavern. The subdued light formed shadows, haunting the limestone catacombs.

The four spheres were connected, forming a trapezoid. Centaur, the leader of our group, held the base of the array. Hornet held the right side. Cone, the left. They swayed to the right. A moment later, to the left. "I can't tell which way it's pointing," stated Centaur. "Sometimes it points this way. Sometimes that way."

Stick supervised the ordeal. The nearly flawless protection his platinum armor provided him limited his mobility. He was an Octagonal Knight, a proponent of Neutrality. Returning balance often---but not exclusively---consisted of defending the unjustly persecuted. "It oscillates between the Dreadful and Grim Mountains. We must be equal distance between the two spheres."

"Which one then?" I asked. I preferred others to make decisions. If I asked the question, I still contributed.

General Paint, by far the shortest member of our company---at 125 sims---was the broadest. He was sturdy, as mentally and emotionally as physically. Spending most of his life in Orpo---the Positive-Order Frontier---he spoke systematically, one thought leading logically to the next, cautiously validating the micro and macro truth of each word. "The Lich mentioned trolls and a drak---a red drak. Don't they both live in the Dreadful Mountains?"

"You're assuming the Lich spoke truthfully," Cone responded. "Something the criminal mind isn't renowned for." Cone was an expert on the criminal psyche. He was once the chief of police of Jasper, a metropolis a few kays into the Negative Frontier. "How likely is it that the remaining spheres would be in the same location? It's apparent, in the manner the spheres are swaying, that they're in different locations."

Hornet said, "We need to choose a direction." His affinity to Gaea manifested in him never being harmed, not directly, or substantially. We looked at him as our spiritual leader. "If we head to the Dreadful Mountains, aren't we guaranteed to find at least one of the spheres?"

"Pulp, what do you think?" asked Centaur.

I didn't like giving my opinion. It put me too much on the spot. Agreeing was okay. Hornet's rationale was reasonable, as where other's. I was beginning to waver. Why did I have to be re-created in Chaos? "I agree," I blurted out before I changed my mind again.

"Then to the Dreadful Mountains and Chaneg we go. General Paint, lead us to the surface. I for one don't wish to spend any more time down here than is absolutely necessary. The sub-arbols may have abandoned their city, but for days or forever?"

"If I can. Under normal circumstance I could guarantee my ability to lead you out, and even approximate how long it will take. The chaotic tangle of natural and artificial tunnels and caverns surrounding us has muddled my subterranean orientation."

"WAAA!"

We turned around. A hatching drak waddled up to us. It was just two days old, but was as tall as me. It had followed

Nimbus, our sentient golem companion, devotionally, like he was its mother. After Nimbus had died fighting the Lich, it had wandered off---we believed forever. We found it---initially---in a geode cave in route to the sub-arbol city. It appeared to have been hatched from the earth. Babies were never born on Limbo. Sterilization was implemented to prevent a society from sustaining itself---thwarted by our unforeseen immortality. Crystal, as the drak babe was called, was the second incidence of implausible procreation. Hornet's wife, Dinga, was pregnant.

"Go away," Centaur insisted. "We can't take care of a drak, especially one as loud as you."

"Maybe we can tie it up and leave it?" Cone suggested.

"I don't believe I could permit that," Stick responded. "If we leave that thing here, trapped, it will certainly come to harm."

"If Gaea wishes it to survive, she will set it free," General Paint stated.

"I think we're going to have to take Crystal with us, until we find someone to raise it," said Hornet

"How many people you know are willing to raise a drak?" asked Cone.

"Gaea will find a way," said General Paint.

"Do you think Gaea appreciates you speaking for her?"

"We all speak for her," said Stick. "Some of us just don't annunciate very well."

Chapter 12

DARKNESS AND TWILIGHT

We began our trek back to the surface. It had taken us a day to reach the sub-arbol city, with us knowing where we were going. How long might it take before we saw sunlight again?

The answer was two hours. We hadn't yet emerged from the earth, but a few rays had penetrated the partially collapsed ceiling of the auditorium-sized cavern in front of us.

"We can't be that far down then," said Hornet.

"Three-hundred and twenty-one meters below the surface," General announced.

"So, it's unlikely we'll be able to climb to the top," Centaur muttered.

"Even if there were sufficient handholds, the ceiling is unstable."

"A rope tied to an arrow?" I suggested.

"Even if you could shoot an arrow that far, we don't have enough rope," said Centaur.

"How much would that much rope weigh?" Cone pondered. "To fight that much gravity, you'll have to shoot it out of a cannon."

"Something's moving," I reported.

"I don't see anything," said Centaur.

"It stopped."

"That probably means it's now aware of us, if it wasn't before," said Cone.

"Is it waiting to strike when we pass?" Hornet questioned.

"Perhaps. Or just hiding until we leave."

"If we're aware of an ambush do we still consider it an ambush?" I asked.

"Is there a bypass?" asked Centaur.

"Not until we enter the cavern," General paint answered.

"Isn't that contradictory?" asked Stick.

"There are obstructions, created by the fallen ceiling. There are many routes, around and through the debris. Some are dead-ends. Others, with patience, will lead us to the other side."

"There's a possibility, then, of us sneaking past that thing hiding," stated Centaur.

Before we could decide what action to take, Crystal complicated matters---or made it simpler, depending on your point of view. Like all children, she was curious. She walked up to the thing that was hiding.

"Do we draw her back?" Hornet whispered.

Before that decision could be agreed upon, she disappeared.

"That was odd," Stick declared.

"Listen," I said. "She's still moving. She didn't disappear. We just can't see her." Some people hated their mutations, but I loved mine. I was tall and athletic. I had the eyes of an eagle and the ears of a wolf. I sometimes bumped my head, but that didn't deter arbols from bumping into me.

"WAAAA!" Crystal bellowed mournfully.

Instinctively, we darted forward to aid her. As we got closer to where she disappeared, our surroundings began to close in on us. Seeing one-hundred meters in front of me, became seventy-five, then fifty. We slowed down, then halted.

"Very odd," said Stick.

"The lantern can't even penetrate it," said Hornet.

"It reminds me of a black hole," said Cone.

"A wall of darkness."

"Not a wall, but a cloud," I clarified. "Look closely. It's irregular, and moving, slowly, but perceptibly---it's billowing."

"WAAA!"

Stick stepped forward and disappeared.

"It reminds me of that time that hole appeared in our hotel room," said Centaur. "Pebble jumped through and we followed."

"That didn't turn out so well," said Hornet.

"Most of us survived." Centaur disappeared.

"That's one way to return to the surface," said Cone.

"I must admit, I'm curious what it feels like to be re-created," said Hornet as he and Cone disappeared.

"I enjoy being a trog," said General Paint. "But duty calls." He also disappeared.

If I died again where would I be re-created? I wouldn't mind returning to the Copper Forest. I shuddered. I was just as likely to be re-created on Manta's island or that bluff where I hacked out that heart?

I expected the black cloud to smell like smoke. It was nearly odorless, with a hint of sulfur: more noticeable than repugnant. I couldn't see a thing. Usually when it was dark, dim outlines of objects could be seen. I saw nothing. Not wanting to bump my head, I bent over, my hands in front of me, using them as both feelers and a shield.

It began to lighten, pitch black becoming a charcoal gray. Crystal was no longer crying out. I continued to walk forward. I bumped into someone. The only person that low to the ground was General Paint. I began to distinguish shapes. I saw Cone, Stick, and Centaur ahead of me. Beside me was Hornet and General Paint. Crystal was in front of us. Something large was in front of her.

"I should have lit a flare," said Cone.

"Could something like that have worked against this kind of darkness?" Centaur questioned.

"It's a pental flare. We sometimes use them in Jasper when nothing else works. They're expensive, so they're only used when the safety of the city is compromised."

"You brought one of these flares with you?"

"No."

Stick went into attack mode, placing his two-handed platinum sword in front of him, like he was praying. I placed an arrow in my bow, as did Hornet. Cone drew his dart revolver. General Paint and Centaur, neither having a ranged weapon, held their respective mace and axe tightly in front of them.

"You can put those away," spoke the large object that was now recognizable as a drak. "We shouldn't provide such a poor example for the little one, should we?" We didn't completely do what was suggested, settling on moderating the aggressiveness of our stance. Crystal stood beside the 40-meter long drak. A talon stroked a smaller version of itself. We eased up even more. "How did this precious thing become your companion?"

"We were present when she hatched," said Centaur.

"Her parents?"

"We believe she was immaculately conceived, and birthed," Stick answered. "Her shell was a geode."

"So, humans, a trog, and a gent find a baby drak? Sounds like the beginning of a joke."

"Also, a golem who was once a drak," Centaur added. "Did you know Nimbus?"

"Nimbus Southern Spine? We wondered what happened to him. I always liked him. I envy the Neutrals, for the balance that surrounds them. I wish I had such balance. I guess I like others to suffer too much. We all have our weaknesses."

"You wouldn't be wanting to be make us suffer now, would you?" asked Hornet.

"Anyone who chooses to accompany two draks deserves to spend a little more time in their present form. Do you like sundim or moon-brighten better? I don't like bright light or darkness. I prefer the balance of twilight. Nothing's more pleasant than being beside a hot fire on a cold night."

"Then why did you attack us with that *cloud*?" asked Centaur.

"Attack? You've may have met a couple of draks, but you

didn't know them if you believe this is all we are capable of doing when we attack. Light occurs more often than darkness---on the surface. To balance light, there must be darkness."

"So, you chose to live in the darkness of the underworld?" asked Hornet. "Isn't that going too far in the opposite direction?"

"I don't live in places of complete darkness. That is why I chose this place---aberration or gift of Gaea---it's become my paradise, my dream home."

Now that the black cloud had completely dissipated, the twilight dragon, as I referred to him, could be seen clearly. Its scales were monochromatic. They varied from black to white, with a majority of them being somewhere in between. Its small arms were an extension of its wings, looking like they belonged on a bat. As characteristic of most draks, its back legs were much longer than its arms. It spent as much time on them, on its haunches, as it did on all four.

A mutual opportunity? I said, "Crystal being a drak, its best she be raised by a drak. You wouldn't know of anyone of your species that might be willing to do so?"

The twilight drak opened its mouth, displaying its dagger-sized incisors. It was either happy, or hungry. "An honor for any drak to raise one of its kind from a hatchling. A loss for you, but best for the drak. Crystal might never be able to eat someone resembling her guardians. If she succumbed, she may feel guilty about it."

"We had similar concerns," Cone responded.

"We best be going now," said Centaur. "You wouldn't mind directing us back to the surface, would you? The most direct route."

"I don't think you want that. The skor are tasty, but astringent, less palatable to mammalian digestion."

"We had the displeasure during our descent," said Cone. "We never had the opportunity to sample the cuisine, their claws and stingers distracting us."

"It's a tragedy that Gaea hasn't given you the same natural protections as I."

"But we don't hit our heads as often," General Paint responded. The drak opened its mouth wide again.

"At the crossing ahead, turn right. I must mention this at the next Gathering, a trog asking a drak for directions."

"I never…." Before an escalation in the…difference of opinion…could occur, we directed General Paint away from the drak.

We hugged Crystal, then resumed our journey to the surface. Without error, the trog led us through the maze of fallen debris into a tunnel on the other side of the cavern.

"Should we have also asked the drak to mine some gold for us?" asked General Paint.

"You said you weren't able to navigate a precise path," Centaur answered.

"Because the exit was too far away."

"The drak apparently knew which way to go."

"As did I."

"Honey works better than vinegar."

"Trog don't season their food."

"You sense any more…delays?"

"That would have been the appropriate question to ask the drak. There is another irregularity up ahead." There was a combination of sighs and shudders. "That doesn't mean something else will attempt to detain us. We might be fine."

"Might?"

"Should? Trogs make poor coaches. False hope circumvents truth. You should be aware, by now, the dangers of the underworld."

A quarter later, General Paint shared a revelation. "The disturbance is new."

"Disturbance?" Hornet questioned.

"Disruption in the fabric of earth and stone. The

irregularity."

"Were you a scientist before you were incarcerated?" I asked.

"Banker."

"So, it was embezzling that earned you an all-expenses paid trip to Limbo?"

"My temper."

"Trogs are renowned for their stoicism."

"A perpetual life sentence gives one time to change his temperament."

"Is this disturbance manmade?" asked Centaur.

"Manmade? No. But, something made it."

"Let's be prepared. If a beast can burrow through stone, it can as easily burrow through us."

We continued forward, but cautiously. "BACK UP!" General Paint barked. The right wall of the gallery exploded. Λ black bipedal beetle emerged behind the debris. We believed the thing was coming towards us, but it continued forward, into the left wall of the passageway. It dug through the rock, its massive claws receiving futile resistance. When it hit a soft spot---where there was more soil than rock---it sped up, like a drill bit first boring through wood, then the drywall behind it. When it came to rock again it slowed down.

About the time we felt it safe to continue, something else emerged from the burrow. It looked like a worm, but was much larger: a meter tall, about five long. Instead of having a single slit for its mouth, it had three that were concentric. It began eating the chunks of rock the beetle's abrupt arrival had created. Whatever nutrients it received from the minerals must have been limited, because it defecated most of it out a few seconds later. Defecated may not have been the most accurate term. Most of the stone passed through it---in a condensed form---like water through a fish.

While the creature ate, three demi-humans, nearly as tall as I, emerged from the tunnel. They looked like gnobs, but with dark hair and pale skin, and dusty gray clothing. It was difficult to distinguish them from the rocks. They carried large picks.

"Brass, stop eating that," spoke one of them. "It will make you sick. You know how ill you become when you eat anything they touch."

"We saw it first," spoke another. "We've been hunting it for over an hour. It may look nice over your mantle, but this one is ours."

"Gentlemen, we can't chat here all day. You know what happens if it forgets it's the prey: we become the prey. Thank Gaea its brain isn't large enough to figure that out most of the time."

"Come on, Brass. You'll get your fill as soon as we catch up to it. Gourmet gravel tastes much better than that sewage you gobble when we're not looking." The gnobs tilted their pewter-looking helmets in our direction, then chased after the creature through the burrow on the left side of the tunnel.

"I'm going to assume we don't need to put *following them* up for discussion," said Centaur. He looked at General Paint.

"We proceed forward."

An hour later we came to that fork the drak warned us about. "Right it is," General Paint uttered sourly.

"How much longer?" asked Hornet.

"To be determined."

"But we are going the right way?" asked Centaur.

"Would you like to return to the drac and confirm it with him?"

We walked through the underworld for hours. Hours became a second day. We camped once, in an alcove.

The location of the next sphere was tested.

"That's comforting," said Cone. "It would have been demoralizing to learn we had spent this much time in the bowels of the earth going the wrong direction."

"It may have been for the best," said Centaur. "How many

things would we have had to fight above? We're in the Negative Frontier. We haven't been in any substantial danger since we left that arbol city."

"They weren't arbols," I insisted.

"Maybe it works differently in the Negative Frontier," Hornet suggested. "We met a lot of nasty things underground in Neutrality and the Positive Frontier. Could the deeper we go here mean the less extreme?"

"The problem with logic is it only works until it doesn't," Centaur responded. "Speculation doesn't warrant a suspension of caution. Double watches tonight, gentlemen."

I was paired up with Hornet. We had first watch.

"Do you think Crystal will be okay?" I asked him.

"As well as she would have been with us---more so. Do you know how to raise a drak?'

"I never had children. I don't think I even thought about them until Crystal came along. You must be thinking about the child you will have, night and day."

"I haven't been here as long as you. Having a child doesn't seem so odd to me, but of all the places to raise one...."

"Gaea works in mysterious ways."

"Do you think Gaea is real, that she's a god?"

"She's just a name we attach to the things we don't understand, but isn't that what God is?"

"So, you think there is a reason Dinga and I are having this child?"

"You saw how that drak reacted. Limbo will change if children are born?"

"Children usually don't save a relationship, just delay the inevitable."

"The moral bulge isn't shrinking. The drak was correct about one thing: Limbo is better off being balanced. If it gets much more lopsided, or even stays the way it is for much longer, this world will fall apart, and I don't mean just emotionally."

"Crystal is the beginning then, the first child?"

"She will infect more than the drak with her innocence."

"So, Crystal is a virus?"

"More like a vaccine. May your child be raised in a healthier world."

"Are people going to change that much?"

"Some might, but the real change will occur when those born dilute criminal morality."

After waking Centaur and General Paint for the second watch, I attempted to sleep, but my mind was too awake. I never believed I would have children. First, because no one would want to have children with me. Later, because I, and the potential mothers, were sterile. What would it be like raising a child, to always have someone rely on you? If Gaea mutated us enough to no longer be sterile does that mean Gaea might also deny us our immortality? For some of us, it was a curse, but for others.... I wasn't sure which group I fell into. It depended on the day. If Gaea gave us a choice between eternity and death, none of us would be tormented or denied.

The remainder of our subterranean excursion was uneventful: no more Dead or drac or hunting parties.

We were getting closer to the surface. The trog didn't mention it, but I could tell by the decreased humidity. If we weren't going to reemerge in a desert, we were going to surface near one. Shortly after I came to that conclusion, the rock began to change. We passed through less granite and limestone, more sandstone.

Chapter 13

HOODOOS

We walked out of the underworld into a forest of hoodoos---slender, erratic rock spires. "Hello." Cone walked up to one of the columns. He halted, abruptly, appearing perplexed. "I thought there was a woman standing there."

"There is," I confirmed. "Back away and look up." Many of the sandstone pillars looked like people. Or animals. Or objects. The hoodoo that confused Cone looked like a woman wearing a loose, flowing dress. The indirect lighting of the mineral forest cloaked the stone in shadows, obscuring details, demanding our imaginations to fill in the gaps. We perceived people primarily, but occasionally a bird of prey or spider or lizard.

The novelty of potential encounters wore off---as did our caution. We retained the positioning we used in the underworld, but more spread out. Cone spent a majority of that time as PROC2, but he began to linger, often falling behind Stick, who was PROC1, the protector of our rears. He became mesmerized by the illusions the stones created. He marveled at how easily someone with so much detective experience was deceived.

The surprised yelp he made saved him---the duration yet to be determined. Stick promptly appeared beside him. Two tall, lanky, extremely flexible semi-humans tore at him with claws and teeth. Their bodies were gray and hairless, contributing to them blending flawlessly into their environment. They wore no clothing, revealing their---apparent---lack of gender. With procreation not possible---with the exception of Dinga's pregnancy and Crystal's birth---it was inevitable genders would ultimately mutate out.

By the time we had all reached Cone, four more of them jumped out from where they had blended in. Cone was in bad shape. He remained on his feet, but he was covered in blood from the incisions that tattered his hide. Stick attempted to block further attacks by inserting his body between Cone and his combatants. The elem-infused armor flawlessly deflected the claws and teeth, preventing not only penetration, but scratches.

We fought back, but not very successfully. Our opponents had extreme regenerative powers. It took seconds for wounds to completely heal---including limbs to grow back.

Centaur wasn't willing to give up. "Try to hack them apart," he suggested. "There is only so much matter they can regenerate." Cognizant it wouldn't matter, I followed his desperate advice. Trolls didn't regenerate using their own flesh. They used free-matter, what changelings employed to transform into a larger form. Free-matter functioned like stuffing for the small amounts of restricted-matter that determined shape and function. The pieces of troll flesh that littered the ground shriveled and evaporated, returning free matter to the ether.

Everything had a weakness---even trolls. But what? Fire? They lived in a desert. Cold? It sometimes got below freezing in a desert at night. Electricity? Probably not. Electricity might shatter stone, but as long as those smaller particles created still existed, however many groupings of them there were, they would eventually reform.

As I fought a troll off with the short sword I used whenever I couldn't use my bow, I thought of all that troll free-matter floating around in the air. My mouth suddenly got a bad taste in it. I had to spit. Smirking, I discharged the rancidness onto its source. It melted a hole in the troll, like my saliva was acid. I expected the hole to immediately fill in---it didn't. "WATER DESTROYS THEM! THEY CAN'T REGERNERATE MATTER CONTAMINATED WITH IT!"

I opened the canteen attached to my waist. I flung its

contents at the troll that was attacking me. It dissolved like rice paper. All that was left of it were its two feet. There wasn't enough water in the container to complete the job. I spit on each appendage. A powdery residue was the only evidence the troll once existed.

My companions, aware now of the devastation of liquidation, also dumped water on their opponents. The trolls withered away rapidly. But there was still one remaining. Centaur declared, "I believe we're out of water."

Cone retorted, "Not entirely." With blood dripping down his hands onto to his arms, he pulled down his breeches. "You'll want to get out of the way." The troll rushed him. At the precipice of the troll grasping him, Cone urinated on it. The yellow liquid steamed as it dissolved the creature.

Cone collapsed.

"Do we have another healing stone?" I asked.

"No," Centaur responded softly.

"He's dead," stated Stick, without emotion.

"May he be re-created without Negativity," spoke General Paint solemnly.

We left Cone's body where it lay. Burial ceremonies were rare on Limbo, a superfluous endeavor when bodies were just temporary shells a soul briefly occupied? Cone's true essence was the elem that would soon be sheathed in another casing.

After finding our way out of the hoodoo maze, we connected the spheres to confirm our destination. "It's just pointing to the Dreadful Mountains this time," Centaur declared.

"Trolls are Chaotic," I said, "so we must be in Chaneg."

"The southern end of the Sabre Desert is Chaotic, so we have at least an approximation where we came out."

"We're definitely in Chaneg," stated General Paint. "My skin is crawling. Being oppositely aligned apparently does that do a person."

"I don't feel anything," I commented.

"You're not completely opposite," said Hornet. "You are Chaotic, as much a component of this region as its Negativity." True, but it did not reassure me. Was I that similar to some of the creatures here?

"The Sun and Sea Road should be to the west of us," said Centaur. "We wish to head south, so let's angle towards it in a southwesterly direction."

Our journey had been a microcosm of one's existence on Limbo. Companions die. New ones take their place. We experience one environment for a short time, then speed towards another. How many more changes might occur before we collect that last sphere?

"FEEK!" I blurted.

"What?" My four companions questioned in unison as they stopped.

"That's Lady Palm's camp ahead of us."

"Women don't frighten me, especially those with class," said Centaur.

"Sophistication wasn't the reason she attached Lady to her name. A lady, she isn't. She uses the title to empower herself, as a man might use Lord."

"Like Lord Coal?" Hornet asked.

"Exactly. Lady Palm is a gent. One of only two women in the Brotherhood. You met Jasmine already. Lady Palm is one of the worse that lives in the Negative Frontier. Biased, perhaps, coming from a male perspective. We assume women are good, so when they aren't, they aren't just bad, but horrid. That isn't the situation here. Lady Palm is truly horrid. She'll do whatever it takes to accomplish her goals. Killing. Seducing. Yes, I said she was willing to do whatever it took. Fortunately, I was never willing to trade with her. Someday I fear she will rule the Brotherhood. My salvation and Limbo's is that she will still only be able to cast one vote. She has gained influence, but can still be countered."

"Shall we detour around her camp?" suggested General

Paint.

"It's too late. Here she comes."

A very tall woman, covered completely in a beige cloth, looking like a mummy except for where she had her eyes exposed, rode upon a gigantic tarantula. It was two meters tall, twice that in diameter. Lady Palm still looked like a child riding a toy car. She was that large. She sat upon a cushioned saddle. There weren't any reigns. She appeared to be using her legs to steer the creature.

"If she was so willing to sell her body for your vote, why does she cover herself?" asked General Paint.

"You are looking at it from an ordered perspective," I said. "There is some logic associated with chaos, but it's inconsistent. She chooses to cover herself, because she doesn't want anyone to see her unless she chooses them to. It's a form of power. If she openly displays herself, she's giving a part of herself away for free."

Lady Palm had an escort. Dozens of tarantulas surrounded her. None of them were as large as her steed, their diameters varying from one to three meters.

General Paint shivered.

"How could someone who lived in the underworld be afraid of spiders?" asked Stick.

"Afraid? I detest them. They're sneaky. Trogs prefer directness. They're poisonous. I hate being sick. Gaea has a proclivity for balancing things out. The largest spiders have the weakest venom."

"Pulp, so nice of you to pay me a visit." Lady Palm's voice was airy, but harsh, like a sandstorm. "You brought some servants with you. When did you modify your position on servitude?"

"They're my companions. We're just passing through. We won't delay your itinerary."

"Plans have a tendency to change. Thank you for bringing your...*companions*." The word was difficult for her to say, like it was new to her, or offensive. "My pets need some practice."

"You'll be sanctioned if you harm me."

"I won't compromise my rise. My pets are aware *you* are off limits."

"I don't believe I could allow my friends to be attacked and not defend them."

"Your choice, of course. If my pets are attacked I can't prevent them from defending themselves, can I?"

"Flee," said Stick. "I'll keep them at bay while you escape."

Centaur immediately countered with, "Together we'll be able to...."

"One poisonous bite could finish any of us. We've used all our penta. No more healing stones. No more protective shields or electrical discharges. This armor should protect me. Worst case, I'm transported to the Octagonal Prism." The Octagonal Prism is where the souls of Octagonal Knights go when their bodies die. Instead of being re-created, a precise replica of an Octagonal Knight's body at the time of their acceptance into the order is reformed around their soul. The soul is recalled to the Prism at the brink of death, bypassing Gaea. An Octagonal Knight never dies. A person must be pure, to have never been re-created, to become an Octagonal Knight.

"Good luck," said Hornet.

"We'll meet you in Badlands City, one way or another," stated Centaur.

"I hate running more than I hate spiders," said General Paint. "But one's duty sometimes involves doing things we don't like. I agree, reluctantly, with the strategy."

There was nothing left to say. After a curt nod we ran off. The spiders chased us. Stick immediately went into action. I shouldn't have delayed by frequently looking back, but I couldn't help myself. Stick swung his sword in wide sweeps parallel to the ground. The blade was knee-high, the perfect level to slice through legs. To be effective, Stick didn't have to amputate all the legs, just two or three on every spider. As the spiders became unbalanced they crashed into one another.

A few of the spiders got past Stick. We were able to dispatch them with arrows before they reached us. Before dropping down the backside of a rise, I glanced backward a final time. Stick was still battling at least a dozen spiders. We debated whether to return, but if we died now Stick's sacrifice would have been wasted.

Chapter 14

TRANCE

We spotted the South Sea shortly before sundim. Feeling relatively safe beside the road that embraced its coastline, we set up camp. We were hesitant about going too far, hopeful Stick would catch up with us. He didn't---that night---so we assumed the worst.

"He found us once," General Paint assured us. "He'll do it again." He was referring to Stick being killed in the Twin Hills and rejoining us in Jasper.

With Stick no longer in our company Centaur became PROC. Another loss and we'll likely have to relinquish finding the final two spheres, at least temporarily.

We headed south on the Sand and Sea Road in the morning. Centaur estimated it to be 100 kays to Badlands City. From there we would head southeast to the Dreadful Mountains.

Most roads had waystations on segments that were longer than a person could travel in one day. There were two between Palm Dust and Badlands City. The first we arrived at an hour into our walk. We weren't ready to bed down, but our water bottles needed to be filled. They were enthusiastically exhausted destroying the trolls. Sometimes there were inns along heavily traveled roads. This road wasn't one of them. The waystation had a single one-room building, a pit toilet, and a well.

We filled our canteens from the well and used the toilet. For a person accustomed to indoor plumbing it wasn't much, but when you're used to squatting in the woods---or desert---it was paradise. We were preparing to leave when we heard a woman's voice. There hadn't been anyone at the way station when we arrived, or so we thought.

"She might be stranded," suggested General Paint. "Better for her to wait for an escort than to travel alone."

"She must be in the building," said Hornet, "hiding in the shadows."

Centaur said, "Let's take a look. I'll go in, alone. A crowd might frighten her." Seconds later we heard, "Anyone in here? Miss? You need any help?"

Two minutes passed. Silence---no words spoken, no movement. I entered to investigate. A young woman huddled in the corner. Tattered clothing barely covered her. She had a sweet, innocent little girl look about her, but she was also definitely a woman. Her dark hair covered most of her face and bosom. Just enough of each was revealed for one to wish for more. Centaur sat on his haunches next to her. It appeared he was attempting to comfort her. The girl turned her head towards him. She brushed her hair away from her head, revealing iridescent blue eyes. It was difficult to look away from them. They drew you in like a ledge of a cliff. Centaur was fixated on them. He appeared dazed. A dagger appeared in the girl's hand. I rushed into the room from the doorway where I was watching as she plunged the dagger into him. Aware now of my prescience, she ran past me out the door.

The armor Centaur wore protected his vital organs. Nothing serious was injured. He looked more surprised than hurt.

"Looks like you're going to survive," I told him. "Infection would concern me, if Gaea didn't abolish it. Bleeding out is our greatest worry." I applied pressure to his gashing wound with the heel of my hand. I smiled at him to lighten the mood. Instead of grimacing, his face revealed a singular state of bliss, his thoughts immersed in something pleasurable he hadn't chosen to reveal.

General Paint and Hornet rushed into the building. "That girl that shot out of here turned into a monster as we pursued her: top half still woman, lower became a quadruped, pads instead of hooves, like a cat or dog."

"We couldn't keep up with her---it---when it began to run on all fours," Hornet announced.

"It likely won't return, not while we're here," I said. "As soon as it noticed me it rushed off. I don't think it's strong enough to attack more than one of us at a time. I'm not sure it would even be much competition for one if it didn't use deceit."

"How is he?" asked Hornet.

"He'll live. The physical injury isn't the problem, although we'll need to suture him soon, before he loses too much blood. Let me see your sword cloth, Hornet." I removed my hand, replacing it with the ochre-stained cloth. "Sustain pressure." Hornet did as instructed. "Anyone sew someone up?"

"An introductory course for a trog," stated General Paint. "Wastes time in the field coming home early to pamper flesh wounds. Got twine in my pack." The trog headed outside.

"He doesn't look like himself, does he?" Hornet commented.

"Like he's in a trance," I responded. "He's completely unresponsive to external stimuli."

General Paint returned with the twine, and a needle. It took him seconds to close the wound.

I smiled. "You've done this before, haven't you?"

"Not that many times. Trogs usually stitch themselves. I'm rarely derelict in my defense."

I wrapped the sword cloth around Centaur, padding it at the wound with another.

"They should die those things red," Hornet suggested. "They would look less gruesome."

"Let's walk him outdoors. Centaur could use some fresh air and sunlight," I said.

"To each his own," said General Paint. "To a trog, dim and musty is sucking on a mother's teat."

Either the exertion, or losing contact with the site of his trauma, snapped him out of it. "She was beautiful, wasn't she?"

"Some of the deadliest things are," said General Paint.

"Where did she run off to?"

"Don't worry, she won't be back," said Hornet.

"She won't be back? Why would she want to leave me? Am I not worthy of her love?"

"She tried to kill you," I said.

"I'm certain it was an accident."

"What is wrong with him?" asked General Paint.

"Those who are in love are said to lose their wits," I said.

"How could someone love someone who almost killed them?" asked General Paint.

"It happens all the time. But his adoration was chemically induced. Love often involves some exchange of pheromones. They're usually not this intense, or sinister."

"They'll wear off, won't they?" asked Hornet.

"Probably, but when? In an hour? A day? A month? The pheromones may have done permanent imprinting."

"Great," said General Paint. "With Centaur incapacitated, indefinitely, we have lost half of our company. An army can't win with half of its troops decimated."

"I believe I can fix Centaur," I said. "I was an herbalist's assistant prior to being re-created as a gent."

"Like what Dinga is training to become?" Hornet asked.

"Nothing so noble as a druid. Most people view any pental creation outside the Wizards Keep as black magic. Those who practice such are called witches and warlocks. The witch I studied under lives in the Herb Islands."

"I remember seeing them on Centaur's map. They're in the South Sea."

"So, we are close to them?" asked General Paint.

"Just a ship's ride away."

"Then let's hire us a ship and find what you need," Hornet suggested. "Dinga was so enthusiastic about herbalism that she forced some of what she learned on me. I might be able to help."

The islands would supply everything we needed. The difficult part would be collecting elem fiero. The only place in the South Seas I knew that had it was near the rim of Curry Island's volcano. I wasn't looking forward to reuniting with Manta. But some things couldn't be prevented. I was already mentally preparing myself for the encounter.

Badlands was a term describing crudely chiseled land, of intersecting shallow canyons, usually within a grassland. Being so close to the coast we never saw such an area. The desert did gradually transition into a grassland. Nearly non-existent at the first way station, sparse at the second, but abundant by the time we reached Badlands City.

Badlands City was a much rougher town than Palm Desert, the last settlement we were in before we entered the underworld. There were no roads in the town except the two intersecting highways. Its buildings were haphazardly placed a few meters away from the ones beside it. Few aligned with their neighbors. From a bird's view, the city must have looked like someone had randomly dropped wooden blocks between the grasslands and the sea. The stunted grass between buildings, if not dead, looked the part. Everything in town was dirty, as conspicuous indoors as out.

We still had some money, so we splurged on two rooms at the *Snake in the Grass*, the finest inn in town---by default---the snakes in reference to the shady characters who chose to make the inn their home away from home. We weren't harassed. Who was foolish enough to confront a gent?

The mattresses were covered with dust. We believed---foolishly---taking off the dirty sheets would make a difference. How did that much dust get under them? Had the inn ever changed them? Baths were delayed. Even if the water was clean---a remote possibility---we feared we would immediately become dirty again.

Chapter 15

PODS

We debated whether to leave a message for Stick with our innkeeper. Was it better to remain anonymous or increase our odds of reconnecting with the Octagonal Knight? We left a note, confidence in an Octagonal Knight improving our odds of success outweighing the possibility of someone---malevolent---searching for us.

We chartered a fishing boat. Fishing wasn't as good on this side of the South Sea. The fish liked being in the Chaotic Negative Frontier about as well as we did. The captain of the vessel snatched our offer of guaranteed profit. The only particulars we gave him were the amount we were to pay him and the duration of the voyage. Living in the Negative Frontier, he was accustomed to ambiguous---and often dangerous---business transactions.

We found that out when we were attacked by what I first thought were seagulls. The birds were much larger, and had the upper torso of a woman. Woman was a rough descriptor. Their withered skin was so badly sun-damaged and wind-burnt they looked like large raisins with shrunken breasts. Their expressions were inhuman---vapid and crazed, like a rabid dog that chased after a stick that wasn't there. They begged for food. The captain swung at them with a harpoon until they left. "Pests."

"Couldn't we have given them something?" Hornet asked. "They look like they're starving."

"If we feed them they'll come back."

"Isn't that what they're doing anyway?" I shot back at him.

"Not as often. They probably wouldn't beg at all if some of the fishermen weren't as diligent. I'm tempted to leave the Jackal Coast."

"Why don't you?" asked General Paint.

"There are *some* good things here. The vices in Neutrality aren't as exotic as those in the Frontier." The captain didn't elaborate.

The only island of ample size in Chaneg was Rosemary. Such a pretty name for a place not so pretty. The island housed a brothel that was so masochistic in nature it was forced to operate remotely from standard Chaotic-Negative activities. Sharing the island, was the village of Piano Forte. The northern shore was sparsely populated. We chose to land there. Harvesting elem-enriched herbs, although not illegal, was still frowned upon.

The Third Time Is A Charm Church had a congregation in Piano Forte. Their most controversial doctrine required a carnal connection with Gaea. I will not go into the details, but they have come up with very creative means to do so. Another belief of many Third-Timers was that only She should manipulate the elements. Anyone having anything to do with elem or penta was labeled a witch. Manta was offended that dabblers in the art were given the same designation.

Having a couple of hours of daylight remaining, we began our elem harvesting. Four blue elem---elem aqua---were required for each healing penta, so our primary harvesting had to come from a water source. With the ocean surrounding us, the potential for harvesting them was endless. The elem-infused urchins I collected off the shore of Curry Island weren't as prevalent near Rosemary--- an entire afternoon wasted.

We slept peacefully on the beach. We didn't hear the brothel or Piano Forte.

"I think we're going to have to seek another source of blue elem." I poked the coals of the fire we used to cook the fish we ate for breakfast. We also ate indigenous fruit Centaur collected for us the night before. We told him his girlfriend needed them. He returned with an armful of colorful fruit. He was beaming, like he was bringing a surprise bouquet of roses.

Centaur became downtrodden. "Where is she?"

"She is taking care of personal business," Hornet replied. Centaur slunk off, embarrassed he had asked the question.

"Do you know what else might contain elem aqua?" asked General Paint.

"Manta mentioned many things in passing. Urchin were so prevalent off the shore of her island that is the only source of elem aqua we harvested. I remember her mentioning a seaweed that became agitated if someone touched it. It would slap at you and entangle you. Manta said she was strangled to death once by a cluster of it. She hasn't harvested any since."

"Understandable."

The captain shoved the last piece of fish into his mouth. Through mumbles he said, "I spotted some of that strangleweed on the way in. If you look real close you can see it floating on the surface. We sometimes fish near it. Most things swimming near it will dart away once they recognize it. Nets fill quickly. Some days fish notice it from further away, which clears an area. Don't know why there's good fishing there some days and other days none at all. It must have something to do with changing currents or tides."

"Do you mind taking us out there?" I asked.

"It's your gold. The weed won't damage my ship."

Harvesting a plant that wanted to harvest you back wasn't

easy. The seaweed was attached to the seabed by a tendril. It received all of its nutrients from the sprawling vegetation that floated on the surface. The tendril was its anchor, preventing the current from transporting it to a less desirable location.

"So, we need to detach it from the seabed?" asked General Paint. "Like clipping toenails."

"How do we do that?" asked Hornet. "Without it strangling *us*?"

"There isn't any vegetation near the base of the plant," the captain replied. "Sometimes strangleweed dislodges in a storm. Sea life loves to nibble on it---after it's dead. It's rich in nutrients from the creatures it digests."

Hornet and I were the ones who had to dive to the seabed to cut the strangleweed free. Centaur wasn't coherent enough, and trogs never went in the water. It was difficult enough for General Paint to be on the ship. We dove underwater along the perimeter of the weed patch. The vegetation stopped about five meters down. A couple of meters below that was where I attempted to cut the stalk. Upon touching it, the stalk snapped, abruptly becoming aware of my existence. The vegetation turned towards me. Leafy vines sought me, coming up short. As soon as the stalk was cut through, the plant drifted away. I rose to the surface for a breath.

The plant convulsed, shaking like a dog in its attempt to dry itself. The churning created waves that lapped against the boat. Abruptly, the weed went motionless. "It's now safe to bring it aboard," spoke the captain. "It's not dead yet, but the shock to its system will keep it immobile until that happens." General Paint used a metal hook to snag it, then drag it into the boat.

Hornet bobbed in the water beside me, empty-handed. "I couldn't hold my breath long enough to cut it through all the way," he explained through labored breath.

We returned to the seabed. After combining for 12 weeds we were both wiped out. We swam back to the boat, barely able to pull ourselves over the railing. We lay on the deck as General Paint collected the last two weeds.

"What do we do now?" he asked.

"When a plant or animal contains elem it's always in the nexus. It acts as a supplemental energy source. It gives it extra vigor. You ever notice a plant or an animal that is considerably healthier or larger than those around it? It probably has elem in it."

"Does something like this actually have a center?" asked Hornet. Each plant consisted of a long strand with branches of vegetation jutting off of it like a tree.

"There's a nodule where the vegetation begins," said General Paint. "It's the only part of the plant that's prominent."

"That must be it." Hornet and I had recovered enough to be able to stand up. "We need to cut it away from the weed. The rest of the plant we can return to the sea."

With three of us working, it took minutes to complete the task. The captain was fascinated with what we were doing. Anything to break up the routine was a vacation for him. Centaur stared off into space, an enthralled grin on his face, clearly thinking about the beautiful, stranded girl he had met at the waystation.

We returned to the island, this time to Piano Forte. I needed a mortar and pestle. The village was pregnant with tourists, from all walks and crawls of life. There were as many brothel visitors as those wishing a more wholesome retreat. And in the middle of it all were Third-Timers proselytizing. The open-air market was abuzz. Everything was sold there. If it couldn't be sold in one store, the one next door certainly had it. There were whips and prayer rugs, chains and beach chairs...and finally a mortar and pestle.

"What herbs would you like to go with that?" asked the proprietor of the store we bought it at. "I have things that will send your mind to distant shores while your body tans on the beach. If you don't want to pay brothel prices, there's an herb that will make any woman you meet think she works there."

"No thank you," General Paint responded tersely.

"My pardon. I also own the spiritual book store down the street. I have a freshly scribed copy of the seventh edition of *What Gaea Told Me You Must Do*. It was signed by the monk of Springwood Abbey who copied it."

"Time for us to go." I held onto General Paint's shoulders, steering him away. He looked like he was about to redecorate the store. It wasn't wise to bring a devout Order Positivist to such a diverse venue.

We returned to the boat. We traveled to the north side of the island where we camped the night before. We placed the weed pods on a rocky slab adjacent to the sandy beach. "Sometimes unexpected results happen when elem-enriched herbs are crushed," I told my companions. "Spontaneous combustion is one such response. We wouldn't want this ship to burn down, do we?" From his shocked, but awed expression the captain definitely didn't, but he wouldn't mind it happening to someone else's ship, from a safe distance.

I began to crush the first pod. The others backed off, anywhere from 10 to 30 meters, depending on their aversion to danger. The ground pod became a stringy paste. I continued to grind until it became fine. I scooped out the paste onto a porcelain drying plate. I immediately started on the next pod. To get the consistency I wanted, it took me 15 minutes per pod. It took the entire afternoon. My hand felt like it was going to fall off. After not blowing up after the first two pods, my companions helped. They gave me a break in the middle of crushing every pod, but I had to do the crucial initial and final grinding myself.

The ones I had crushed early in the afternoon were already dry. "How do we know if they contain elem?" asked Hornet.

"Manta used a device that looked like an elem collector to test each herb." Hornet retrieved an elem collector from his backpack and handed it to me. It was the one that had been used to collect elem fiero in the Sabre Desert. One red dot was displayed. "I don't think we want this anywhere near blue elem.

When elem combine to form penta worse things than spontaneous combustion can happen." Hornet snatched it out of my hand and replaced it with an elem collector that was empty.

I swung it in front of the now powdery substance. There was a faint flicker of blue. "I think we got a winner." I carefully scraped the powder into a small ceramic bottle and stoppered it. I tested the next dried sample. Nothing. Then the next. Three of the twelve specimens contained elem. "It looks like we're going back out tomorrow."

Hornet appeared perplexed. "Why can't we collect elem directly, like Dinga did?"

"This is the way I know how. I can create a Disease Healing penta relatively safely with my method. Can any of you make such a guarantee the other way?"

The third day of collecting we attempted a shortcut. I tested the strangleweed before I ground it. None of them tested positive. Either we had terrible luck or the elem collector couldn't penetrate through the pod membrane. If true, that would have also prevented us from collecting the elem directly. The elem Dinga collected wasn't trapped in anything. They were found floating in the air or water, or on the ground. More crushing and grinding. Three additional positives. Considering our history with needing elemental assistance, the extra wouldn't go to waste. I swore I would never become an herbalist again after what Manta deceived me into doing, but there were times during the elem harvesting and processing I considered returning to it. As with most things, elem could be used for good or for evil.

"Now we need one red elem," I said after I stoppered the last bottle. "I don't think I can safely combine the elem Dinga collected with those I harvested. We're going to have to collect one ourselves."

"Didn't you say the only red elem you were aware of in the Herb Islands was on the witch's island?" asked General Paint.

"We either have to go there---or back to the Sabre Desert. Being unfamiliar with the plants that may contain elem, it will be a lot of trial and error."

"Would you be willing to return to Curry Island?" asked Hornet.

"Willing? Possibly---as a last resort. I didn't want to apprentice myself with a witch, but at the time it was a necessary sacrifice."

"But one you now regret."

"I don't believe curing Centaur is a choice I will regret."

The captain wasn't as enthused about going to Curry Island as he was going to Rosemary. But he had enjoyed the last three days---paid to not fish, with a bonus of doing some things he never dreamed about doing. We encouraged him by doubling his pay, providing him several more days of leisure or adventure. He accepted the money, with token grumbling.

Chapter 16

REVENGE

Living on Curry Island as long as I did, its geography was etched in my memory---scarred might be the most accurate way to describe it. There was a way up the side of the cliff without having to fight off worms that attacked you from their burrows. We weren't able to circumvent the crabmen. But they had a weakness, becoming effectively impotent once turned over on their backs. The captain suggested we use the net poles. Being bipedal---the crabs---it was much easier than anticipated. We didn't have to flip them. We simply had to push them hard enough for them to lose balance. As we climbed the steps up the volcano, six exoskeletal monsters cried out in frustration as they tried to right themselves.

We attempted to circumvent contact with Manta, as unlikely as that may be. The lichen on the lip of the volcano's crater could be reached without passing the witch's keep. The three of us made quick time up the mountain. Centaur, the captain, and crew, remained on the boat. We had a job to do, and as soon as we collected our specimens I wanted nothing more to do with the witch's isle---this time permanently.

We scraped eight of the lichens into the collection sack. It was more than we needed. The extra was cautionary. Did I mention that I never want to return to this island again? I typically took only two or three at a time to not overgraze, but I no longer cared for the survival of something that assisted with the survival of the witch. With surprising ease, we returned to the ship. Where was the witch? Could it be that she wasn't aware of us? Might she even be dead?

"Can we leave now?" asked the captain. The longer his boat laid anchor off the shore of Curry Island the more nervous he became. He became quite anxious when the crabmen finally turned themselves over. They looked towards the ship. A translator wasn't necessary to relay their desire to murder those on board.

"Not yet. If I'm not back by sundim, I probably won't be coming back." I returned to the shore, tipping crabs as I ran towards the steps that would lead me up the cliff. Why did I suddenly want to see Manta so badly? Curiosity? Revenge?

"WE'RE COMING TOO!" yelled General Paint, still on the ship. So unexpected was my departure it took a moment for my companions to react.

"No. You will only get in the way. Manta will use you against me, as a distraction. Wish me luck."

"May Gaea protect you."

Manta was waiting for me. "Have you returned with what I asked you to collect?

"It's been 20 years."

"Once I have the specimens, I will teach you the remainder of what I know."

An elemite entered the room. It delivered an herb, then left. "There are so few of them that haven't worn out. My collections have never been so low."

Something snapped. Seeing the elemite reminded me of what I felt when I tore out the dripping heart from the watcher and learned it had once been a person, that the souls within the watchwood had been become elemites. I attacked the witch with my dagger, attempting to cut out her heart like I did the watcher's. At the threshold of her non-existence I was struck from behind. I had forgotten about the bone golem. As I lost consciousness I heard the witch cackle, "You have learned much from me."

I woke adrift in the sea, but what sea? I straddled a piece of driftwood. What were the odds it would be here when I was re-created? Did I instinctively wrap myself around it before I awoke like it was my mother? Did Gaea curse me or save me? I've heard of people being re-created in the ocean. Most of them drown before finding land. Some of them are re-created numerous times in the middle of one of the four seas, drowning multiple times until their morality modifies enough for them to be re-created on land. Why does Gaea allow that to happen? I've never heard of people being re-created in the middle of stone or in the air. Why would Gaea allow us to be re-created in water? Was it symbolic? We who choose to drift through life are re-created drifting through water?

Land was nearby. It was a small island, just a few hundred meters across. Vegetation grew on it. There might be food and water. If not, maybe I'll be re-created on the mainland.

Once on dry land I examined my body. It didn't appear to be

modified, but sometimes mutations were internal.

I looked up at the sun. From its position I could tell where the center of Limbo was---it being directly below the sun. I could to a lesser degree determine how far away from it I was. In this instance, about the same distance away as when I died. It was possible I could be in one of the other seas, but they would feel different, being closer to one of the other moral extremes. That meant I was still in the South Sea, which meant I was, at best, re-created in Neutrality. I had killed an innocent and become Chaotically Positive, but after attempting to kill someone evil I reverted back to Neutrality. If Gaea existed in physical form, she would live in the Chaotic Frontier.

It didn't take me long to search the island. The only thing I found edible were coconuts, but they were too hard to open. I looked for a rock to smash them. No luck. I walked into the water. Maybe there was something in the shallows.

My search was short. Black talons pulled me under. There were three of them, creatures nearly my size, but more suited for water. They had webbed feet and hands, and gills on their necks. What I first thought were talons were actually black fingernails. They also had black teeth and hair. Their turquoise bodies were sleek, except for a prominent thatch on top. Their eyes were a truer green than their skin.

Not expecting to be forced underwater, I hadn't taken an extra breath. My lungs began to burn earlier than they would have if I knew what was coming. As I opened my mouth to suck in what wasn't available, I began to choke, then panicked. Two of the sea creatures clutched my arms. The third hit me with the butt of the spear he carried, knocking me out.

When I returned to consciousness I was still underwater. Why hadn't I drowned? Water passed through my mouth, down my throat, out through slits in my neck. Why hadn't I noticed them earlier? Gaea hadn't completely abandoned me.

Our destination was a sunken ship. It was intact except for a large hole in its hull. Its elongation indicated the ship likely grazed a submerged rock, tearing the wood like it was flesh. I saw less than a dozen of the aquatic hybrids. I was finally released after we entered a cabin, its décor suggesting it once belonging to the ship's captain.

The creature behind the desk was the most adorned of my captors. In lieu of clothing, the creatures were heavily tattooed. Horrendous scenes of destruction were displayed as rudimentary drawings on their bodies. My imagination connected each illustration with the real-life event they represented.

"I told you to bring me any hu you found on the surface," spoke the leader in the muted, echoing manner sounds were carried underwater. "You brought me a gent."

"It looks hu," spoke one of those who captured me.

The leader shook his head, what a parent might do when his children did something foolish, then turned away to look at me. "What are you called?"

"Pulp Weedwood."

"Pulp will do. I don't care where you came from. Where you're going is what matters. My name is Incision. I'm the one that makes all the decisions. You're probably wondering what we are. We're sea ogres---sorgs. We once looked more human. It wasn't Gaea who implemented the redesign. The sea witch...." I shivered. "So, you know of Manta. Good. That might motivate you in what we have planned."

The sorg had been the crew of the sunken ship. Manta did not actually sink the ship, but she took advantage of the travesty. She saved most of them, but not to return them to civilization, but for her own sinister purposes. She had a Gaea complex. She was compelled to manipulate the world around her. In particular, people. The crew of the ship were to be the canvasses on which she created. The sorg weren't her first design, but they were her most successful.

"No one wishes to be manipulated, physically or otherwise.

One day we will enact our revenge. To accomplish this we need someone from the surface."

"What do you want me to do?"

"There are limitations in how long we can be out of water. We don't have enough time to go to the witch, so she must come to us."

"And you think I can accomplish this?"

"She doesn't have to come all the way to the ship, just to the beach."

It wasn't that I didn't wish to enact my revenge on Manta. It just didn't seem possible I could do what was asked. How was I able to make Manta do anything? I don't think she went down to the beach the entire time I was her assistant. What might make her leave her keep?

"I have a plan that might work. The last thing I want to do is return to Curry Island. For retribution I'll make the sacrifice. Just point me in the right direction."

"We'll do better than that. We'll escort you."

"You don't need to do that. I have a long, bad history with the witch. I want to hurt her more than I want to escape from you."

"True, but the escort is not only for our benefit. There are things between the ship and Curry Island that don't take contact with others well."

The frontiers contained the most extreme mutations on Limbo. I felt safer being accompanied by six armed demons, but not completely safe. Spears could do only so much damage. Mutations are infamous for taking the normal activities and traits of people and animals and transferring them to settings they didn't originally belong. A pack of sea wolfs eyed us as we passed through their territory. They looked like a child had tore apart his toy animals and connected the upper part of a wolf and the lower part of a seal together. The creatures acted like wolves, most noticeably, when they growled, but they lived in the sea.

The next things we saw were naturally mutated. Human

corpses floated on the surface of the water. Bloated, decayed bodies that somehow stayed intact. "What's preventing them from being consumed?" I asked.

"Someone is protecting them," one of my escorts replied.

"To save a portion of their humanity?"

"To save them for their self. Look over there." On the far side of the corpses, I spotted five creatures that didn't look much different than the bobbers beside them. The main difference was their features had become more grotesque. Their nails had grown into sharp talons. Their tongues were forked and had become as long as snakes. Their eyes, instead of being milky white, were ablaze---red, swollen and seeking. They looked like they belonged to someone with a hangover who wasn't too happy about being disturbed. Their flesh looked like it was rotting, but it also appeared vigorous, like someone was badly injured, but was beginning to heal.

"Are we safe?"

"As long as we keep our distance. You know how a mother protects her young if someone gets too close to them? The same is true for the corpses the ghouls protect. It must be feeding time." The ghouls attacked a corpse. With the precision of a deranged surgeon, they ripped apart the decayed body. Their forked tongues acting as small hands. They pulled away pieces of very tender flesh, flesh that had been marinating in the sea---the world's largest stew pot---for weeks. When they got down to the bones, they split them down the middle with their claws. Their tongues probed inside for the candied marrow. I vomited, then swam hastily away, to prevent it from floating back on me.

"Will they hunt the living when their stock of corpses runs out?"

"Most definitely, but they won't consume them until they are ripe. You see that larger corpse? It was once a sorg, until he got too close to the ghouls' garden. That was just a week ago. They probably won't get to that one until the others are consumed."

"I don't see any fish floating. Don't they like seafood."

"Apparently not. There has been more than one occasion when a shark or a pike or a killer whale invited themselves to lunch. The ghouls, with their talons and ferocity, made quick work of them. The only time they touched the bodies was when they escorted them from the area, so they wouldn't contaminate their food."

"Aren't you concerned about your safety once their stock is consumed?"

"We are, but our immediate goal is to enact our revenge. War with the ghouls is inevitable. We won't leave our ship. They won't leave their garden, as long as it's stocked. It's their ship too."

"I was wondering. So, they were part of your crew?"

"As were the corpses."

"And you don't get along anymore?"

"Mutation didn't just affect them physically. The ghouls have become deranged. And the corpses are just...dead."

We swam for a couple more kays. We stopped at a stony outcropping that protruded ten meters out of the water. "We call it Border Rock. It marks the boundary between Neutrality and the Chaotic-Negative Frontier. The stone used to be on the border---its precise location---but Chaos and Negativity has gained a bit since our ship was attacked by Manta. The difference between the two moral regions is subtle, but it is there. The light is brighter on the other side, and the activity beneath the water more mellow."

"Too mellow," spoke another sorg.

"So, you actually prefer to be a part of the Chaotic-Negative Frontier?"

"The Frontiers are more alive. Neutrality is relatively safe---but boring. Some people like riding a roller coaster: the high rises, the sudden descents, the possibility of death. Others like to spend their entire lives on flat land, where textures never fluctuate."

"Doesn't Gaea have a big hand in it? What one becomes?"

"She does. But we have an equal part: nature and nurture.

And on Limbo we do a lot of self-nurturing."

Curry Island had been in sight from the ship, but once we passed Boundary Rock, it seemed to leap out at me. I had a plan how I might draw Manta away from her keep. If it didn't work, who knows where I might be re-created this time. Even if it did work, she still might be able be kill me.

One of the sorgs made a pained sound. A ship was anchored offshore. My heart leaped. They were still waiting for me. Then I saddened. I can't return to them now. Look what I've become? Even if I hadn't turned completely Negative, I'm with a group of creatures who had. We swam to the far side of the beach, as far away from the unchanged and trog as we could.

"With luck I'll return by the end of the day."

Their response as they headed back to the ship, "With luck our ship wouldn't have sunk, and the witch wouldn't have experimented on us."

As slyly as I could, I ran to the where I could ascend the mountain. At the base of the volcano I looked towards my companions, for possibly the last time. That last transformation hadn't affected my visual acuity. I saw Hornet, General Paint, the ship's captain---and Centaur. From the manner in which he moved it looked like he recovered. Maybe it was all worth it then. I couldn't blame them for my predicament. I was the one who chose to confront Manta. We could have just left after we harvested the lichen.

My ex-companions stood on the beach, about 20 meters from where the ship was anchored. Centaur fell. The others turned around, towards the sea, and began attacking something---more than one of them, whatever they were. They were lank, almost stringy, and pitch black, like the bottom of the sea. Centaur was back up. Water churned fervently as the creatures of land and water fought over the boundary between. General Paint hacked off one of the creatures' arms. A moment later a stub began to grow, within minutes becoming a new arm. THEY WERE TROLLS! But they lived in the sea, not the desert. How were they going to defeat them this time? I had to help them. No, they were no longer part of my life. I was no longer like them. I had to enact my revenge. With renewed determination I hopped up the stone steps, as those who had been my companions fought for their lives.

Manta wasn't surprised to see me. "Have you returned with what I sent you to collect?"

"How could I have possibly returned to the Gibwoods in the short time I've been dead and re-created?"

"Why else would you return to me? There are other ways to become rid of you than by having my henchmen kill you." She was so confident. My plan just might work.

"I have come to bring you information you might find beneficial. Those you have experimented on, the ones from the ship, will attempt to attack you."

"As expected, as your attempt to attack me."

"Wouldn't it be wise to do something about it? There are a dozen of them, much more of a threat then I have ever been. The battle is inevitable. If you choose the time and place, you'll have the advantage."

"In my keep I choose the place and time of my battles. But there is another variable. I still want the watchwood hearts. You wish me to leave my keep so I might become vulnerable. You believe I won't be powerful enough if I do so. I will destroy the sorg, as you wish. But in exchange you will complete the task I have asked you to do."

"What guarantee is there I will follow through on my end?"

"If you don't, the promise unfilled will eat away at you. After years of self-loathing you will bring what I requested, as a desperate act of emotional self-preservation. Do you agree to bring to me what I desire in exchange for the termination of the sorg?"

If I was to rid myself of the witch I had no other option. As long as she continued to live, my existence will be damned anyway. "Agreed."

Manta began making preparations before the word was completely out of my mouth. She took vials of powders from her dusty shelves and carefully combined them. One by one she sprinkled them into vials filled with purified water. Even more carefully she stirred the vials, then placed them in the many pockets of her gown.

She left her laboratory without fanfare. I followed her through the twisting catacombs. Most of the way the grade was steep, but not too steep to be unsafe. We must have traveled a kay by the time we entered the hidden cove at the base of the volcano. The boat was barely larger than a rowboat. Oars were its propulsion system, with the bone golem doing the work. Manta briefly went down to the small cabin in the boat's hull, then returned with a mouth full of dried fish.

"How can you eat at a time like this? Aren't you even a little concerned?"

"Let's just say I have safeguards. I don't plan on dying today."

What did she mean by safeguards? How could anyone truly be safe? No matter how powerful a person she was, she could still die. Maybe not permanently on Limbo, but still painful, and inconvenient. Did she believe she was going to be re-created in her keep? My entire plan rested on her hubris. Was she even more self-confident than I gave her credit for?

The sorg attacked before we reached the ship, either too anxious to wait, or they didn't want the only home they had to become desecrated. I don't think they planned on their battle being so close to the corpse garden, but that is where the two parties intersected.

Manta had uncorked a vial and swallowed its contents. Electricity was discharged from her fingers. It struck a sorg, and apparently the water adjacent to it. Fish floated beside the charred husk.

Manta swallowed another elixir. Light reflected off her at an odd angle, like she was encased in glass. Two spears were harmlessly deflected a meter in front of her. I dived into the water, a precaution to prevent an incidental injury. More spears were deflected. Did the sorg believe if they continued to throw them some of them might get through? The shield she created couldn't last indefinitely, but likely longer than that.

But wishful thinking wasn't the only reason the sorg continued to bombard the shield. As she watched from the front of the boat, two sorg climbed into the back of it. The witch hadn't noticed them. Unfortunately, the bone golem did. More unfortunate was the sorg not being aware the golem's artificial intelligence wasn't complex enough for it to modify the rowing command it was given. One of the sorg responded verbally to it being seen. Manta swallowed another elixir as she turned. Both sorg leapt, one at the golem, the other at the witch. Attacking a pile of bones with a spear wasn't very effective, especially when the pile of bones attacked back. The golem couldn't attack without instructions, but it was able to intuitively defend itself. The other sorg had an even more difficult time. The energy shield was replaced by a cylindrical wall of flame. The attacker became an inferno as he made contact with the witch. He ran to the edge of the boat and leapt off, flames following him. The water doused the flames, but not soon enough.

I watched the action from where I maintained my position in the water. If I saw a weakness somewhere that I could take advantage of I would add to the attack, but I saw none.

Manta's next trick was more sinister. She had the golem row closer to the corpses. She shook one of her vials violently, then threw it at a corpse. It broke as it made contact. She repeated the process three more times. The corpses began to move, first in an abrupt jerking motion, like someone had started their hearts, then more naturally. "ATTACK!" the witch shrieked. An animated object follows the simple commands it is given. The first voice it hears is the voice it will continue to follow until the penta that powers it expires. If someone had been more aware what the witch was doing, they may have been able to sneak in a command before she could initiate the assault.

The remaining sorg had their hands full. One might think fighting a corpse was easy. It was true that being dead they didn't exhibit much creativity in their attack, but until they run out of energy, killing them was impossible. Unlike trolls, what was detached from them didn't grow back, but it still took a while to tear apart something that was trying to do the same to you.

An additional adversary had entered the scene. The ghouls didn't appreciate their food supply suddenly reanimating and swimming off. If they were going to lose most of their crop they intended to plant another. The sorg's demise was inevitable. I still couldn't conceive of a way to succeed, so I remained immobile.

The witch must have had similar thoughts, because she eased up on her attack, and her defense. She was stunned---literally---when a large hammer stuck her head. Somehow Hornet, Centaur, and General Paint escaped the clutches of the trolls. The trog had the honor of incapacitating the witch. To not be out down, Centaur chopped at the bone golem like it was a stack of wood. The kindling he created was in too many pieces for the golem to retain its animation.

Chapter 17

ELIXIRS

As General Paint was preparing to deliver the fatal blow I yelled, “WAIT! I don’t think destroying her body will actually kill her.”

Hearing my voice, my friends rushed to the side of the ship I hovered below. If their smiles were any wider they would have decapitated themselves.

“I knew we would find you,” said Hornet.

“We all did,” Centaur insisted.

“Not ‘til you saw him on the boat.”

“How were you able to escape the trolls?” I asked.

“Everyone---thing---has a weakness,” the trog replied. “It’s the duty of a tactician to find that weakness and use it to his advantage. *Sea* trolls, being the opposite of *desert* trolls, it was logical if water destroyed one, the lack of water would destroy the other.”

“Being out of the water didn’t kill them, but it prevented them from regenerating,” stated Centaur.

“We just had to draw them out of the water,” said Hornet.

“Hornet volunteered, his Gaea-like ability to not be harmed minimizing the danger to him.”

“It was more like I was running for my life. Realizing I was going to tire before they did, I turned and struck one. Noticing the incision didn’t immediately heal, I notified the others.”

“It helped that the trolls didn’t become aware of their weakness until we had nearly wiped them out,” said General Paint.

"The last one fled into the sea. Trogs don't swim, so I had to let it go. It may have been the last one---so there may not have been anyone for him to inform---but I still would have liked to come away with a clean mission."

"Then we saw you in that boat," said Hornet.

"I wish we would have seen you sooner," Centaur apologized. "When did you first see us?"

"I...."

"Pulp probably couldn't even tell you," said Hornet. "It must have taken all his wits just to survive."

I didn't inform them of me ignoring them when they were first attacked. Was I a coward? Was I selfish? Did it really matter now that we were all safe and the witch captured? What were we going to do with her? "I believe Manta has a bell jar in her keep---something that will retain her soul when she dies, to safeguard it from fleeing and mutating."

"So, we can't really kill her," said Centaur. "Doing so will just return her to her keep."

"How can we be rid of her without killing her?" asked Hornet.

One of the few surviving sorg emerged from the water. It appeared to be their leader. "I have a plan. Bind the witch, then give her to me. She won't die, but she'll wish she could."

"I won't allow anyone---even this monster---to be tortured," General Paint insisted. "Gaea forbids it."

"That's your interpretation, possy." Possy was a derogatory term for someone from the Positive Frontier. Possies are the bleeding hearts of Limbo, their self-perceived good deeds superseding common sense. "She chose to torment, so she should be tormented. That is equitable. Are you insinuating Gaea isn't fair?"

"In a perfect world we would not be having this conversation."

"But we don't live in a perfect world."

"Manta needs to be stopped from ever harming someone again," I said.

"I don't like giving someone to this thing any better than you," said Centaur, "but we must do whatever we can to prevent Manta from maintaining her hobbies. I'm not saying you should abandon your morals, but sometimes there is a lesser of two evils." Centaur removed the remaining vials from Manta's pockets, tied her up, then threw her overboard.

The sorg was vigilant in preventing the witch from drowning. We followed him as he and another of his kind carried her away. We left the corpse garden behind. The ghouls must have had mixed emotions. They had lost much of their crop, but there was the anticipation of consuming new bodies once they ripened. They were busy collecting the fresh corpses, planting them in the center of the older ones. Older corpses, although tastier to the ghouls, were less appetizing to others.

The sorg carried Manta to the top of Border Rock. They removed her gown. They tore it into shreds, using the pieces to tie her to the rock. Potentially titillating, but not for a woman who lived too hard for too long. Seagulls weren't even tempted to visit. "We'll reinforce the cloth ropes with sea substitutes when they begin to deteriorate. She'll be fed periodically. It's too good for her, but we don't want her to escape by dying, do we?"

As the boat pulled away from Border Rock, the witch began to stir. The Chaotic side of me wanted me to stay, to see her reaction. I didn't have confidence the sorg could keep her prisoner indefinitely, but even a reprieve from the witch made Limbo a better place.

Not having enough time to return to Badlands City before dark, we spent another night on Rosemary Isle. Before sundim we foraged for fruit. It may have appeared to be a tropical paradise from the beach, but inland it was a dark, dank jungle. Typically, the denser the foliage meant the denser the wildlife. Being closed in on all sides, including above us, generated an uncomfortable handful of minutes. The animal sounds were layered. There were so many of them we couldn't tell if some of them came from the same creature, or all were unique. In the jungle there wasn't much time to react to an attack, so we left our bows on the boat with the captain.

Having my sword, the one that looked like a dagger relative to my size, instead of a bow, saved me from an additional re-creation. The spider that leapt at me was a mottled green, a natural camouflage that helped it blend into the jungle. It was immense, but that wasn't why it was so lethal. The edges of its meter-long legs were as sharp as machetes. Sharp, but not particularly strong. With some well-placed strikes I shattered the bony appendages.

I was able to walk back to camp, but upon seeing my friends---successfully laden with bananas, dates, and mangos---I collapsed. I was In bad shape. If someone wished to find the spider I had slain that had to only follow the trail of blood.

"Time to use one those elixirs." Centaur carefully transferred Manta's vials from his backpack to the sand.

"Two, actually." Hornet kneeled down beside him and began to examine the vials. "One to heal his wounds, and another to restore his energy. We're not going to want to wait a week or more for him to recover."

General Paint also examined the vials, but from a standing position. He was short enough that his eyes were about the same level as Hornet's. "The symbols aren't traditional."

"Pulp, do you know what these mean?" asked Centaur. I struggled to lean up---unsuccessfully.

"I'll describe them to you." Hornet picked up one of the vials. "This one has circles and a chevron." He set it down and picked up another. "A cross." He picked up a third. "A dash."

General Paint let out the breath he was holding. "So, no souls, no black elem?"

"Unless one of the other varieties is missing," Centaur

added.

"That's one of the things I like best about being ordered---few unlesses."

None of the symbols sounded familiar. "I'm sorry. Manta was very specific in what she wanted me to do. She didn't share any information she didn't have to. I never learned her symbols."

"I wish Cone was here," said Hornet. "But maybe the four of us together can figure it out. Being as possessive as she was, Manta wouldn't have created universal symbols. She would have created them for her own benefit."

"She never had proper training," I commented. "I don't believe she was even aware of the Wizard symbols."

"A circle is never ending," said Centaur. "It ends where it begins, everything mixing together."

"Water. A circle must represent blue elem."

"A dash, a segment, is the opposite of a circle," said Hornet. "Linear thinking compared to circular thinking. What's the opposite of water?"

"Fire," said Centaur. "Water is defensive. Fire is offensive. So, a dash must represent red elem."

"The cross represents life," said Hornet. "Not a soul, but the physical nature of something---the matter. So, a cross must represent green elem."

"That leaves the chevron for yellow," said General Paint. "Chevrons are used to represent arrows, to indicate direction and movement. I use them in battle plans."

"Now let's see if I remember what Dinga taught me about penta creation," said Hornet. "We need four blue elem, and one yellow, for energy. We should fortify your strength before we heal your wounds. Your body is the vessel for the healing, so the healthier you are the more efficient the healing, and the less likely you'll die from the shock." Something I never considered. People do die on the operating table, sometimes from things they didn't go into the hospital for.

Having the elixirs pre-mixed was time efficient, but more dangerous. What might happen if the vials broke and combined? Would there be a loud, violent explosion? Would we all grow two heads?

I swallowed the elixir. My body surged with energy, like I was plugged into an electrical circuit. I felt like getting up, and was even in the process of it, before I was pushed down by six hands. "You'll open those wounds," said Centaur. "Wait until all of you is healed." I swallowed the second elixir, the one with four circles and a cross on it. My muscles flexed and contracted. I itched, all over. My wounds began to seal, from the edges inward. By the time the itching and the uneasiness was over there wasn't even a scar on my body.

I got up and danced. Maybe no one else called it dancing, but I jumped around a lot, swinging my appendages wildly.

The condition we were in, relative to a few days ago, put us at ease, providing a restful sleep. Stick might even be waiting for us in Badlands City tomorrow.

Chapter 18

TRAVELERS

Stick wasn't waiting for us in Badlands City. None of the innkeepers had seen him. We had a difficult decision to make. Should we wait for the Octagonal Knight, or head towards the Dreadful Mountains without him? We now had a healthy company of four. If one was foolhardy to traverse the Limboan wilderness, a minimum of three companions was recommended---one person to watch each direction.

"I say we wait for Stick," said Centaur. He had been with the Octagonal Knight the longest, many years before the expert swordsman became a *Defender of the People* by being a *Proponent of Neutrality*. It wasn't surprising he would advocate waiting for his friend.

"We should go on," General Paint insisted. "To delay will give the enemy more time to react."

"Will a few more days make that much of a difference?" asked Hornet. "The Wizards may not even be aware of us."

"I agree with General Paint," I said. "It could be weeks before Stick arrives, if at all."

"He'll return," Centaur maintained.

"Think of the things that could happen between now and then? In a span of days two members of our party died, you were stricken with love-sickness, and I was held captive, after dying, then nearly dying again." I had felt uneasy since my last re-creation. I thought it had to do with being captured, first by the sorg, then by Manta's schemes. But since my escape and healing the uneasiness hadn't dissipated. What was I now? Neutral or Negative? I had to keep busy, to distract my thoughts. It was time to do something. I didn't wish to wait another day, definitely not weeks.

"We all have our reasons to linger or leave," said Centaur. "We mustn't allow one man's opinion to hold us back, including my own. Hornet, if you also think we should leave tomorrow, we'll go. If anyone can catch up to us---alone---it's Stick."

"If I knew when Stick would arrive...but we don't. We need to reach the next sphere as fast as possible. I have a wife waiting, and a kid on the way. I would rather spend my time in the Raspberry Mountains than in Badlands City."

"That decides it then," said Centaur.

"Stick is our friend too," said General Paint. "But he is a warrior. He would not want our mission to be compromised waiting for him."

It was an arduous trek to Amber, the closest settlement on the Trail of Dread. Most people hearing the name begin to sweat and twitch nervously. But there was a segment of the population that was enthused with the rugged peril the name envisioned. It was 190 kays to the town. The first third of the journey was through the badlands, a twisting, shallow canyon maze of unruly earth. It was rumored that when the Chaotic-Neutral Frontier expanded to accommodate the multitude re-created into that morality, Gaea hadn't quite figured out how it would work. The badlands were the result of her first attempt.

The Trail of Dread was, for the most part, constructed above the canyons. There were just a few instances when the road dived into the twisting maze. We were particularly cautious when that occurred. We traveled single file, with General Paint retaining his position as SCOUT. Hornet was ART1. I, ART2. And Centaur, PROC. Being the strongest, Centaur was the best suited to protect our rear. It also gave him time to determine what elixir to use if we were attacked. Five of them remained. Unfortunately, the only healing elixir we had was a Cure Disease. Only concerned for herself, Manta had taken with her a single vial of each of the healing elixirs. The others were evenly divided between offense and defense.

We typically travelled 50 kilometers a day. But not today, with the uneven rolling terrain. Hornet believed we did 40 before sundim. I insisted it was 30. General Paint said it was 36. Which Centaur confirmed when he pointed to the keystone beside the road.

"So, that's what those numbers are for," said Hornet.

"What else could they have been used for?" Centaur questioned.

"Self-guiding tour markers?"

Centaur wasn't sure if he should laugh, but he couldn't help himself, which infected the rest of us, even General Paint, to a lesser degree. Just what we needed after a long day, the first of many into the most dangerous region of Limbo.

We spotted a pack of bipedal jackals earlier in the day. There were just three of them, so they left us alone. Later in the day, or maybe the next, they would stumble upon a party weaker than us. We also saw harpies, hovering like vultures. They also didn't risk an encounter with us. How many altercations did we repel each day? How many more times would we be attacked if there were just one or two of us? How many more confrontations might we repel if we had another couple of people with us, one of them being an Octagonal Knight?

We camped beside the Trail of Dread on a knoll. It was flat enough on top that we were able to pitch a tent and build a fire. It was argued whether we should make camp in a more secretive manner. It was decided that those who wanted to hunt us would find us, be it in the open or hidden in a ravine. We could see into the canyon directly below the knoll, but that was about it. The twisting catacombs hid things too well.

I had first watch. I compared the badlands to that area we entered when leaving the underworld. Cone died there. Who might die here? I thought about death more since my last re-creation. When one mutated considerably, dying on Limbo was more like really dying, not just being reborn. Was Gaea responsible for that, or did I do that to myself?

Nothing attacked during the night. As a consequence, we woke rested, ready to resume our journey. Our second day and night in the badlands was just as uneventful.

An hour into our third day we could see the horizon, a sparse grassland replacing the irregular gorges. An hour after that we met the first people we've seen since Badlands City. The couple was heading in the same direction, but at a more leisurely pace. They were adequately provisioned for a short journey, but barely prepared for a violent encounter. They each carried a dagger, in a scabbard, but neither had armor, not even leather. Leather armor reduced bruising from blunt attacks, and sometimes prevented slicing attacks from reaching skin, but for intense hand-to-hand combat it was practically useless. The woman wore a dress. The man, slacks, a button-down shirt, and a cloak. They each carried a pack. Neither was large enough to store a tent or a substantial bedroll.

"Good day," spoke the man after we caught up with them.

"Do you live close by?" asked Centaur.

"We live in the Glen of Lights. We get bored staying in one place too long so every month or so we go for a walk."

"You don't appear to be adequately provisioned to spend the night," spoke General Paint.

"Trogs feel naked without their layers, don't they?" cooed the woman. "How can one experience a different place if they sleep in the same tent every night?"

"Aren't you concerned about things attacking you in the night?" asked Hornet.

"And a thin layer of canvas will protect us from these things?" asked the man.

"Do you wish to accompany us on our journey to Amber?" asked Centaur. "We could slow down a bit if you can't keep up with us."

"We can move quite swiftly if we choose," spoke the woman. "We walk slowly because we wish to enjoy the scenery."

"We would enjoy the company if you don't mind," spoke the man. "We don't meet many people."

"Are you going to Amber?" I asked.

"Sure. We can go there."

"It can become lonely sometimes," the woman added.

Introductions were giving, then the six of us continued our respective journeys, together. The woman was called Twig. The man, Beak. They had an ambiguous relationship. At times they appeared to be mated. Other times more associates than friends.

Midday we came upon an irregular rise of land. It looked

like the badlands, but in reverse. Instead of having ground gouged below, the land shot awkwardly upward.

Beak said, "It would be wise to circumvent the Scabs."

"Is that what those hills are called?" asked Hornet.

"Seems appropriate to me," General Paint commented.

"The creatures that live there look similar to us, but they're scaly like a lizard," spoke Twig.

"They aren't particularly difficult to thwart, individually," added Beak, "but sometimes they all attack, 20 or so of them."

The road branched prior to reaching the base of the Scabs. The more heavily traveled fork detoured away from the hills. The other fork appeared to be the natural continuation of the Trail of Dread. Grass had grown over parts of it. If it hadn't been so straight it might have been overlooked.

We had another 30-kay day. Thirty-five to be precise, if the kaystones could be believed. The flattening terrain was offset by our sluggish travelling companions. One-hundred and eleven kays since Badlands City. Another 80 until we reached Amber.

After eating we went to bed. To guarantee we reach Amber in two more days we needed to leave early the next day. The couple volunteered a watch shift, which Centaur declined. Risking hurt feelings for security was a no-brainer for him. Our traveling companions didn't appear to be offended. I had the first shift. Twig talked to me most of the time. She asked me questions about myself, and what I planned to do in the future. I was careful not to mention our attempt at reconstructing a portal. Beak appeared to be awake the entire time, but he spent that time away from the conversation, staring at the moonlit hoodooed horizon. Hornet took my place after an hour.

Twig asked him the same questions she asked me. She was the most inquisitive person I had ever met.

I was woken by General Paint. It was still dark. "Our two tag-a-longs are gone." Hornet was also up, looking as groggy as I felt.

I looked around. "Where's Centaur?"

"Over there, at the edge of camp---asleep. I found him like that when I woke."

I walked over to Centaur, as did Hornet. We both shook him. "I tried that already," said the trog. "He doesn't appear to be harmed, except for not being able to wake. His breathing is steady, as is his heartbeat."

"So, our traveling companions weren't the helpless innocents they led us to believe," Hornet commented.

"That we led ourselves to believe," I said. "Why sedate Centaur? They didn't harm anyone or take anything."

"We don't have anything that will pull him out of it, do we?" asked General Paint.

"Time," I suggested. "I don't think they put him in a coma. He is just sleeping soundly. The sedative should wear off---eventually."

"How long is eventually?" asked Hornet. "How long do we wait? The sedative may have been given to him to force us to stay here longer than we intended."

"Why wouldn't they have just killed us in our sleep, then?" General Paint questioned. "Staying here until he wakes is safer than attempting to carry him the rest of the way to Amber."

Centaur woke at moon-brighten, completely unaware of what happened to him during the night. "The last thing I remember is going to bed after my shift. I feel so foolish allowing those two to do what they did to me. Exactly what did they do?"

"They put you to sleep." I examined Centaur in more detail now that he was up and it was light. "There are two puncture wounds on your leg."

Centaur felt the small wounds that were already beginning to heal. "I wish Cone was here. He might be able solve this mystery. It seems so odd. Pulp, do you think you'll be able to track them?"

I examined the perimeter of the camp. "Amber still appears

to be their destination."

"That's convenient for us," said Centaur. "I wasn't looking forward to deciding whether to follow them or continue to the Dreadful Mountains."

It took me less than a quarter to lose their tracks. "They just vanished."

"Did they just fly away?" questioned General Paint.

"Not that far-fetched," said Hornet. "Dinga has that ability."

I returned to the last footprints I was confident belonged to them. "Lots of prints---human and animal. The ground is hard enough here that if someone stepped lightly on another's print it may not increase the depth of the indentation."

"So, it's possible for them to still be on the road," Centaur hypothesized.

"But for how long?" asked Hornet. "A few meters, kays, or indefinitely?"

"I'll watch both sides of road for prints that spur off," I said. "It's going to slow us down." There was no argument, or counter proposal, so I did what I suggested. Ten minutes later I got frustrated and gave up. Many animals crossed the road, but there wasn't any evidence humans did.

We sped up, to make up for the time I wasted. Our goal of 40 kays was achieved, and then some.

Chapter 19

BLACK

We contemplated pushing through into the night, but commonsense overruled exuberance. It was never wise to travel in the Negative Frontier at night.

Midmorning the following day we entered the Jaundice Forest. The trees looked like they were dying. They were sickly yellow, tinted something between green and brown.

"They look diseased," Hornet commented.

"Or not getting enough water or light," Centaur added.

The forest was very quiet. Usually a woodland was full of life. There was practically no movement at all. No squirrels skittering in the canopy. No rabbits or deer running across the forest floor. The few birds that were seen were far overhead and flying swiftly, wanting neither to touch the trees nor be near them longer than they had to.

To the right of the Trail of Dread, pockets of water began to form. If possible, the trees within the water and on their perimeter appeared even more sickly.

"That might be the cause of the woods' poor health," I said. "If trees become too waterlogged they eventually die. This whole area probably floods during the wet season."

"Don't some trees thrive in these conditions?" asked Hornet. "There aren't just dead trees in swamps."

"Terraforming is imperfect."

"Wouldn't nature correct the problem eventually?" asked Centaur. "It's been more than a century since Limbo was created."

"I think a contaminant was introduced into the area," suggested General Paint. "If the conditions were always so bad how did the trees originally grow? The byproducts of our mining had inadvertently poisoned the subterranean flora, a couple of times."

"Twice?"

"Apparently there is a statute of limitation on learning from past mistakes."

"Doesn't sound very orderly to me."

The trog frowned, frustration superseding indignation.

"Will we be safe?" asked Hornet.

"We're heartier than plants, and they didn't die overnight," General Paint replied. "It took days before they became sick, and weeks, possibly months, before they died."

"I don't plan on spending that much time here," I said. Spending a majority of my life in the Weedwoods and the Copper Forest I was exceedingly disturbed by the condition of the trees. It wronged me, on a personal level.

Centaur became agitated and excited. "I THINK I SEE BEAK AND TWIG!" Something was moving, far-off into the woods, at least a hundred meters away.

"We're not planning on chasing them, are we?" Hornet inquired. "I'm not sure it's safe to be so far away from the road. It might be a trap."

"The infant is suggesting caution?" Centaur commented.

"I'm married now."

"This might be our only opportunity," said General Paint. "Smelt while the fire is hot."

"I'm usually the cautious one," said Centaur. "But under these circumstances I believe we do need to pursue them. I'm more curious than upset what they did to me. I don't think our association with Beak and Twig is over. If we capture them our next meeting will be of our own choosing."

Military men often react prior to thinking. Conditioned

responses improve efficiency, but not always benefit. General Paint rushed into the woods in the direction Beak and Twig were seen. His movement was the catalyst we needed to make a decision. He was 10 meters ahead of us when we began. Our longer legs caught up to him within seconds. We lost sight of them, but heard movement. We went deeper into the woods.

"DOWN!" General Paint warned in his loudest whisper. From our belly and elbows we saw bi-pedal frogs in crocodile hide armor carrying a wooden shield in one hand and a metal short-sword in the other. They were the same height as a trog. Their gait was a step-hop, looking simultaneously smooth and awkward. The two-dozen or so of them were moving perpendicular to our prior movement. It was unlikely they would see us if we remained prone.

"Could they have been what we saw from a distance?" whispered Hornet.

"When they're out of sight we'll head back to the road," Centaur whispered back.

A minute later General Paint gave us permission to rise. We cautiously worked our way back to the road. Hornet squawked. He was yanked into the air by an ankle. He dangled 10 meters off the ground, swaying from the residual motion.

"These woods must be full of these booby traps," I commented.

"We need to get him down quickly," said General Paint. "Unless they're deaf they'll be here in seconds."

Being the tallest, and the most comfortable and familiar with trees, I volunteered to climb into the tree to cut Hornet down. The others watched, with weapons readied. "You're not going to have a soft landing. Ready?" It was awkward leaning so far over to cut through the rope, but I was successful.

Hornet's fall was padded by the accumulated debris on the forest floor, but not enough to prevent an ankle from being turned. The frog warriors were within sight. Centaur became Hornet's crutch. The manner in which the two of them moved nearly matched those following us.

We may have been able to escape them---they weren't moving particularly fast---if one of us wasn't hobbled. They were slowly gaining. We were going to have to make a stand and fight.

General Paint paused. "Pulp, you and I will hold them off while Centaur assists Hornet." Dissension was balked when Centaur began moving again. Did he believe it was a great option? Unlikely. But it was the best available.

A moment later he stopped. Second thoughts? "There's more coming this way," Centaur announced.

"They're not the same things," said Hornet. "They look more like lizards."

General Paint ran towards Hornet and Centaur. I closely followed. "Left flank." We did as the trog instructed. Instead of following us, the frogs continued forward. They had spotted the lizards.

We turned to watch the outcome after arriving at what we determined a safe distance. The lizards, instead of using hide, used bones as armor. The long narrow yellowing pieces were tied together vertically, resembling personalized fencing. Instead of swords, the creatures carried pole arms, spears with sharpened stones embedded in them, giving the weapons the ability to not only pierce, but slice. It was a brutal battle. At least half of the combatants on both sides were killed. There was a complete lack of fear. Brutality reigned. Limbs were hacked off. Bones were crushed. Gradually, the frogs gained an advantage. Once the surviving lizards were outnumbered two to one they fled, but not happily. Commonsense must have taken over. It wasn't as fun without an opportunity for success. The frogs, instead of chasing after them, began to feast, and not just on the lizards. It was too gruesome to watch.

We headed in the direction we believed the road to be. Limboans had a good sense of direction, but we needed a reference point. In the chaos of making our escape we lost track of our many course changes. We knew north, south, east, and west, but if we were actually here, not there, we could shoot past where we wished to go.

Odors were frequently unpleasant in areas with standing water. They began to get worse.

"Sewage?" Centaur suggested.

"Too astringent for sewage," said Hornet.

"It reminds me of vomit," I said. "Bile."

"I can barely tolerate it," said General Paint. "The odors within the earth are more neutral. Subterranean rock and earth is mild. I don't want my tombstone to read: *The Great General Paint Died From Stink*."

"It's as strong as skunk musk," said Centaur. "It has permeated…everything."

"Whatever is causing the stink must be also making the vegetation sick," said General Paint.

"And we must be extremely close to it," said Centaur. "I can't imagine the odor getting much worse."

A grotto below a large cave was the apparent source of the odor and sickness. The water wasn't just dark, but black. The trees surrounding the pool were poles, their leaves and branches corroded so much they had fallen off. Many of the trunks were broken off, some near their tops. Others closer to the ground. There were as many stumps as spires. The entire area looked like it had been in a forest fire.

"Things are floating in the pool," stated Hornet. Those recognizable: bipedal frogs and lizards, deer, and a large owl.

"It's like the ghouls' corpse garden," I said. "But these creatures aren't as well preserved. Look at their flesh. Most of it has been eaten away."

"Like the pool is digesting it," added Centaur.

The few mosquitoes that had pestered us upon our approach became a swarm. We slapped ourselves and each other, coating our clothes and skin with black and red patches.

"I thought flies were attracted to bad odors and mosquitoes to sweet ones," said Hornet.

"Are those snakes heading our way?" asked Centaur. "I've never known them to group." There were dozens of them, of all sizes and colors. Centaur rummaged through his backpack, withdrawing one of the vials. "Four crosses and a chevron should create a barrier." Centaur swallowed the contents of the vial. After his body went through the characteristic twitching of elem emulsion, he made a circular motion with his arm. The earth rose in front of him. It began to envelop us. Centaur made another circular motion, this time with his hand stretched in the direction of the reptiles. The wall turned, beginning to surround the snakes instead of us. By the time the earth finished growing it was over five meters tall and had completely sealed in the snakes. "I almost trapped us instead of them. I need to remember that penta is a tool. If I don't use it properly it won't do what I want it to do."

Abrupt motion erupted from the cave. Water from the black pool flowed into it. Something had entered the water and was swimming through the pool towards us. A 40-meter-long drak, as black as the pool, burst out of the water. It landed beside us.

"What does it take to make you leave me alone?" it said. Its voice was harsh and bubbly, like its throat was full of phlegm. "Most things don't like the musk, or seeing bodies half-decomposed. Most will flee from mosquitoes and snakes. You would rather comment about them."

"I have a bad ankle," said Hornet.

"Will you leave NOW, or do I have to spray some musk directly on you?"

"Can we ask you some questions first?" asked Centaur.

"Aren't you aware that drak are something to be feared?"

"We've met a few," I said. "Some have been pleasant."

"Pleasant? That's a first. A runt gent calling a drak pleasant. Aren't you aware that my kind and yours are mortal enemies?"

"I've made friends with a few draks."

"I'm the one who's Chaotic and I have to make sense of all of this? It isn't fair. Because gents have an inferiority complex they must group together to defeat a single drak. Obviously, we don't appreciate being attacked. Drak on the other hand don't bother anyone unless we are bothered first."

"And what floats in this bog once bothered you?"

"Damn right. Anything that comes within five kays of me bothers me. I don't even like the scent of other things, so I have to spray my musk to freshen the air."

"You do realize your musk is killing the trees," spoke Hornet.

"The only dead trees are those beside my pond. The others have just been modified a bit. Don't you agree that pine needles and flowers are too sickly sweet?"

"You must have been more of a beer man than a wine connoisseur when you were human," General Paint commented.

"I couldn't stand that girly stuff. It was like I was drinking concentrated fruit juice. I've always enjoyed a pinch of bitterness and oomph more."

"Well, your musk definitely has that," commented Hornet. "More of a slap, though, than a pinch."

The black drak was temporarily distracted. There were those people, when passing a chocolate store, who had to go in and sample some. This drak felt the same way about partially dissolved bodies. It stretched its neck out over the pool and bobbed for dinner. It snatched one of the bipedal frogs with its teeth, then plopped it on the ground in front of it. In three bites it consumed it.

"Pickled frog. One of my favorites. Pickled anything is good. I wonder what pickled trog would taste like."

"We are too stringy."

"Initially, perhaps, but anything that floats in my pond long enough becomes quite tender in a week or so."

"Now that we are finished sharing recipes, maybe you could answer those questions." Centaur was focused, wasn't he?

"And why would I choose to do anything for you?"

"Because as soon as you do we will leave you alone in your rancid kingdom."

"Maybe it would be quicker just to add you to my pond."

"We have more penta than that barrier I created."

The drak sighed, flooding the air with fumes that almost caused our stomachs to empty. "All right, but make it quick. At least one of you smells like cologne, and it's giving me a headache."

"Did you see a woman and a man, both human, pass through here within the hour?"

"You think I just sit out on my front porch and watch people walk by all afternoon? You are the first humans that have come near me today. Is that all?"

"What's the quickest route to the Trail of Dread?"

The drak did its best imitation of a laugh. More noxious air was blown our way. I couldn't help myself this time. I bent over and vomited.

"If you're going to do that, don't waste it. Aim for the pond. How can someone brave enough to look a drak in the eye get lost?"

"The odors here makes one lightheaded," said Hornet.

"They are intoxicating, aren't they? Okay, I'll point you in the right direction. I'm tempted to send you in the wrong direction, but that would make it more likely you'll return. The Amber River is directly south. When you reach it, go left. It will lead you into town. It's not the quickest route, but you shouldn't get lost again."

"We will leave you now," said Centaur. We began walking in the direction the drak suggested.

From behind us we heard, "You sure you wouldn't want to take a swim in my pond, trog? If you taste good, I'll be quite complimentary of your race." General Paint chose to let the comment slide.

Chapter 20

WOLVES

The sun dimmed as we reached the banks of the Amber River. Forty more kays to town. Half what we had at the start of the day. Not bad, but less than we wished. We were determined to abandon this dark, stank place. And it was getting darker. The stink, it was persistent, except for the escalation beside the black pool.

The Amber River achieved its color from its sediments, accumulated, initially, at its headwaters, high in the Dreadful Mountains. There looked to be a road on the other side of the river. Even if the water wasn't so murky, it was foolhardy making such a crossing at night.

The river had a sulfurous odor. Our proximity to it masked the drak's musk. Not the most pleasant experience, but better than the alternative.

The perpetual full moon shined brightly through the skeletal canopy. The trees were becoming progressively healthier, but not yet to the extent they were able to provide a defense against light or rain.

We debated whether to camp at this slightly less depressing part of the Jaundice Forest or walk through the night. Deciding what tooth to pull would have produced more enthusiasm.

Centaur becoming ill resolved our indecisiveness.

"I'll feel better after we pitch these tents," stated Hornet. "The dangers---and smell---will remain, but even-tempered self-delusion will provide some relief. It feels like we're climbing a hill, with the peak not yet in sight. We may never make it to the top, but we might make it to the next rise, after we catch our breath."

As we unpacked our gear in preparation for setting up camp, Centaur's face began to contort. He tore at his clothes, like they were on fire. His armor was thrown to the ground, then he ripped off his tunic and britches. His body contorted. His bones moved tightly against his skin. The hair on his body grew and became denser. His face elongated. His ears grew upward, to a point. He had trouble staying erect. He fell to the ground. His legs began to shrink. A tail formed above his buttocks. It pushed through the top of his underwear. He tore them off. He was no longer human. The transformation persisted until resolving into something resembling a wolf. He growled. At us? Or the situation? He ran off on all fours.

"That doesn't happen every day," stated Hornet.

"Is he coming back, you think?" asked General Paint. "Or are we going to have to chase after him?"

"If he stays in that form I don't think we'll ever catch him if he doesn't want to be caught," I said.

"So, we camp here and wait for him to return?" Hornet enquired.

"Do we have another option?"

So that's what we did. We already had to carry Cone's gear, and partially, Stick's. An Octagonal Knight's armor and weapons dematerialized with his body. What he had in his pack we easily distributed among us. We considered leaving it in a bank in Badlands City or hiding it somewhere, but with the uncertain of returning to it, we chose to retain it. If Centaur didn't return to us in human form, we may have to leave both his and Cone's possessions beside the Amber River.

Centaur didn't return until morning. Still in canine form, he looked disheveled, and exhausted, like he had been running madly all night. He was simultaneously hesitant of us and antagonistic. We placed some dried fish in front of him. He darted towards it, snatching and running. Away from camp, but within sight, he lay down and tore at the food with his razor-sharp teeth.

"Is there anything we can do to force him back into being human?" asked Hornet.

"The state ought to be temporary," I said, "like the sleeping sickness. In time he should change back on his own."

"If he doesn't?"

"I've never heard of a person mutating without dying," said General Paint. "If someone was able to achieve a permanent mutation without Gaea's help that would be quite an accomplishment."

"I think I can help." Twig suddenly appeared in camp. I prefer to think it was due to a mutational stealth ability, instead of us not paying attention. I was determined for it to not happen again.

"I think you've done enough already," stated General Paint.

Twig whined in the back of her throat. Centaur obediently walked up to her. She scratched his back.

"Where's Beak?" asked Hornet.

"It was time for us to part. We had been together for many years."

"Do you intend to make Centaur his replacement?" asked General Paint scornfully.

"Centaur needed something special in his life. The rest of you have either an exotic mutation or family."

"Did you discuss this with him?"

"Speaking with him, his intentions became apparent."

"Quite a change you forced on him based on assumptions," I said.

"There are means to permanently make him human again, if he desires. Lycanthropy is a disease. It can be cured."

"Then let's change him back, NOW," General Paint demanded. "We still have that Disease Healing elixir with us, don't we?"

“Centaur may not want to permanently return to his human form.”

“I don’t believe he is in a rationale enough state to make that decision,” said Hornet.

“Then we need him to transform back into his human form---temporally, at least---don’t we.” Twig began to undress. She had nearly accomplished the task before we realized what she was doing. We turned around as hastily as we could. After hearing a grunt, a mild one, like someone was stretching, we turned back around. There were now two wolves. They were nearly identical. One was slightly larger, and darker. The smaller, lighter one communicated with the other through a series of growls and barks. The other growled and barked back. The tone of the smaller dog was consistently calm. The larger dog was becoming progressively agitated. After becoming excessively so, the smaller dog smacked its paw against the other’s head. It yelped, covered its head with its paws, then backed away a couple meters on its belly. With sad eyes it looked up at the other dog. The smaller dog continued to speak calmly. The larger dog wagged its tail.

The smaller dog began to transform. We assumed it was Twig, because only a female could make a male cower like that. Centaur was already hen-picked. Bitch-pecked may have been the better term, but that word, although accurate, had too many negative connotations to be used in polite company. We turned around again before the transformation was complete.

After providing ample time for her to redress, we faced Twig again. Centaur was in human form beside her. Neither was wearing any clothes. We turned around again. Seeing a woman naked was bad enough, but a naked man beside her made seeing her in that state doubly inappropriate.

“Sorry,” she said. “I’m so used to having just Beak with me that immediately dressing wasn’t necessary. It itches for a few minutes after transforming. Having clothing chafing my skin makes it worse.”

Centaur looked as agitated in human form as he did in canine. "Where did you put my clothes?" We pointed to his backpack. We packed up his gear when we came to the conclusion he may never return. "What happened to my underwear?"

"You did that yourself," General Paint answered.

Centaur found his extra pair. It took him seconds to dress, including putting on his armor. He and Twig continued to scratch.

"You still have that Cure Disease elixir, don't you?" Hornet asked Centaur. "It'll prevent that from happening to you again."

"Why would I want that? I felt more alive last night than I had since...forever. I ran where I wanted to run. I did what I wanted to do. There was no schedule, no plans. I could do whatever I wanted. My energy didn't diminish until the morning. I was famished, but I recovered after I ate."

"Did your senses change?" I asked. "When I became a gent, I could see a greater distance and with much better acuity."

"My hearing and eyesight did improve, but it was my sense of smell that became acute. Once I began to learn the scent of certain things I was able to determine what direction they were in and approximately how far away they were. As I lay on the ground with my eyes shut I could determine the location of everyone. You were in front of me. General Paint, behind you. And Hornet, to my right."

"What was it like returning to human form?" asked Hornet.

"Very unpleasant, both the process, and having to leave the new form I began to love. I followed Twig's lead. She's a great teacher, but in canine form I think I was also more susceptible to being taught. I'm not positive I can return to my other form without assistance. Twig, will you help me when that time comes? Tonight, perhaps?"

"By then enough time will have passed for you to safely change back," said Twig.

"Won't he just turn into a wolf again when it gets dark?" asked Hornet.

"That just happens the first time. Lycanthropy is a disease. Sometimes when people are inoculated by a vaccine they become mildly sick from the virus, because the vaccine contains a small bit of the dead virus. Centaur changing into a wolf was his reaction to being inoculated by me."

"It sounds like you believe infecting him was doing him a favor?" General Paint questioned.

"He appeared to be very happy as a wolf."

"What right do *you* have to make that decision? Would it be okay then if I had physical contact with a woman---of a romantic nature---without her permission?"

"I imagine she would tell you to stop if she didn't wish your attention."

"Being infected is not like asking someone out on a date. It's like being raped."

"That is a Positive reaction to what happened. You are in the Negative Frontier."

"I'm still curious how the mutation occurs," I said. "I know it's like being infected by a virus, but shouldn't the effects be temporary?"

"They are. Centaur and I can't remain in canine form indefinitely. Five hours is about the limit---half a day. If we don't force the disease to go into remission by then, by changing back, it will cure itself."

"How does it return? How are you able to transform into a wolf again?"

"Think of lycanthropy as being a disease that can never be cured, a disease that remains in one's system, that has periodic episodes of reoccurrence. Lycanthropy is like herpes. Instead of the sores reappearing, a wolf does."

"So, Centaur will have a reoccurrence? He will turn into a wolf again?"

"If he doesn't change into one after a certain amount of time on his own he will eventually be forced into that form. I don't think he would be able to go that long without the excitement of being a wolf. It's rare to have a forced change."

"You mentioned there was a danger if one was to change into a wolf too soon after returning to human form," Hornet remarked.

"The canine form strains a human body. We are still human, but with the ability to change form. We aren't changelings, who are permanently mutated into more than one form. If the strain on the body becomes too great the body will die."

"We have an important mission to accomplish," stated General Paint. "We need to get a move on before we waste any more of this day. Good day, madam."

"Oh, I'm coming along. Haven't I told you? When wolves mate they mate for life."

"You didn't?" General Paint was shocked. People living in the Order Frontier only did what they were permitted to do. This didn't sound like one of those things.

"Mating has many connotations," Centaur explained. "Twig and I did have intimate relations last night, in the way dogs do, but we also formed a bond."

"Which you will break when one of you gets tired of the other," Hornet commented.

"Considering the life expectancy of dogs, Beak and I spent many lives together."

"What was Beak's reaction to you abandoning him?"

"He chose to permanently become a wolf."

"So that means...."

"Beak is probably dead now. Over time, his feelings for me changed. He hung on to the ideal of being one's mate, rather than actually being one. We traveled together, but apart."

"He committed suicide?"

"He'll likely be re-created in the form Gaea should have given him."

None of us were too happy about the situation, but we

didn't want to lose Centaur. We wouldn't be together if it wasn't for him. He was not only a friend, but the leader of our company, the one who held us together as our members changed. He helped us come to a consensus when we differed on what we should do. Problems were always caused by a woman. It was the same old story: woman bites man, man changes into werewolf.

We arrived at the town of Amber at the end of a very long day. Two days actually, considering we didn't get any sleep the night before, first looking for, then worrying about Centaur. If possible, the 2000 souls and the structures they lived in looked gloomier and scruffier than the dying flora that surrounded them. It felt like we were walking the plank as we crossed the river into town---figuratively and literally. The bridge was constructed of wooden planks.

As one went deeper into a Frontier the characteristics of its morality became more pronounced. Rudeness and a lack of consistency permeated the town. If a person didn't offer you anything, materially or emotionally, they were ignored, passively or actively. On more than one occasion I saw someone walk on a drunk passed out on the ground rather than walk around. It was said that men without mothers or wives around would wear about anything, or nothing at all, if they weren't told what was proper. There was an abundance of both mismatched clothing and nudity. The few women in the town were treated badly, which the women reciprocated. Without a sense of order, people openly urinated and defecated in the street. With the possibility of an animal once being human, there weren't many beasts of burden on Limbo. In Amber there were almost as many of them as people. If possible, they were treated more poorly than the people treated each other. The only constructive commerce in the area was from the mining industry, centered in the Dreadful Mountains, and their foothills, the Troll Hills. Barges laden with ore and stone were moored to the numerous docks. When emptied, oxen would pull them back upriver. The ready supply of stone from the mountains, and the lack of quality wood in the Jaundice Forest, demanded most of the buildings be manufactured from stone. The structures were crudely constructed. There were gaps between many of the stones, with some of the holes large enough to see through. If the climate wasn't so temperate that may have been a problem. What was a problem, was the lack of personal hygiene. Relative to the visual and olfactory stench bombarding me, the sea ghoul corpse farm became a fond memory.

The inn we stayed in, the *Gold and Granite*, had rooms that hadn't been cleaned in years, including the sheets. We fled, not caring if we received a refund. Escaping the inn was more crucial than the money we would have fought over. After restocking our supplies, we walked two kays in the direction we intended to travel the next day, then set up camp.

General Paint pulled Centaur aside. "You haven't told Twig about the portal, have you?"

"We are a mated pair. I tell her everything. She assured me she wouldn't pass on the information. Wolves are loyal to their pack, and we---you, Hornet, Pulp, and I---are now her pack."

"I didn't want to offend. It's just that we'll soon be in the core of the moral bulge. Trustworthiness isn't one of the pillars of Chaos."

Centaur patted the trog firmly on his shoulder. "None taken. Having two people along who can turn into wolves will be a blessing. You'll see."

That evening Centaur and his mate transformed, and went wandering. I had second watch. They returned before I woke General Paint. They lay beside each other panting. In the manner they watched the woods I felt they were giving me permission to turn in early. When I awoke they were lying beneath a blanket together, in human form.

Chapter 21

MONKEYS AND SHEEP

The Trail of Dread turned almost due east after it intersected the Amber River. It paralleled it along its northern bluff. The oxen that pulled the barges upstream left evidence of their passing. On one occasion or another all of us stepped into the green and brown gunk.

The vegetation became more verdant the closer we got to the foothills---and farther from the drak's musk. Broadleaf transitioned into conifers, initially pines, then into firs and cedars. The air became humid. Moss became prevalent, coating trunks and branches. Some of the ferns were as large as small trees. It became almost pleasant---if we didn't have so much on our minds.

The worst of the worst were supposed to live in the Dreadful Mountains. How difficult was it going to be to acquire the next sphere? Trolls were rumored to possess it. We have encountered them twice. Neither group had been amiable. Would we also be able to discover a weakness for the group that possessed the sphere and be able to take advantage of it?

I also worried that I was re-created on the wrong side of the boundary. Was I really that Chaotic and Negative? Was revenge a form of chaos? Wasn't it logical---fair even---to do something bad to someone if they did something bad to you? What did revenge get me? I died and my friends had to rescue me, nearly dying in the process. Was perpetually paying and repaying a perceived wrong logical? That wasn't very orderly. I was definitely Chaotic now, but was I also Negative?

The Trail of Dread steadily diverged from the river as it began to climb. Twig halted us. "It's too quiet. I can't smell what's ahead in this form." She began to strip. "No," she said as Centaur began to follow her lead. "It's too soon for you."

"But you're going to change."

"I've had more practice, dear. The strain will be too great for you at this time."

Twig handed Centaur her clothes as she removed them. Accustomed as we now were to the transformation, we adverted our eyes automatically. A moment later a shaggy wolf bounded past us up the trail. Twig was briefly out of sight, but by the time Centaur had stored her clothes and had placed her small pack on a shoulder, she returned.

She made a quick series of low growls. "She says there are monkeys ahead, a large troop of them," Centaur translated. More growls. "There are few animals in the direction we travel. She suggests we be as wise as the wildlife."

"Monkeys?" Hornet questioned.

"The Limbo version of monkeys, with a Chaotically-Negative disposition."

"Is there another way into the mountains?"

"The Trail of Dread is the only approach from the west," I said.

"Now what?"

"Monkeys don't frighten me," stated General Paint.

Twig growled again. "She says there are many of them. A hundred angry bees are deadlier than a single crocodile."

"She was able to say all that in those yips and grunts?" Hornet queried.

"Approximately. Many of the words a wolf speaks have different meanings in different contexts." Twig wasn't done. "She has come up with a plan I think might work." Centaur growled back at her in a pleasant manner. Her response wasn't so kind. He hit her nose. She backed away, whimpering. She lay on the ground, looking up at him with eyes that flung daggers. "A wolf can travel much faster than a man, or a monkey. We'll distract them as you walk past. Twig wanted to do this alone, but I insisted I also change form. She is concerned that my body will react poorly to me changing at this time. I insisted that with two of us we could look after one another, and that my will power and constitution was strong enough to survive the change."

"Couldn't we just wait until the monkeys move on?" asked Hornet.

"Do you know how long that might be? Hours? Days? I'll be okay. I won't stay in this form longer than is necessary."

Centaur changed into a wolf before we could formulate a logical counter to his proposal. Hornet, General Paint, and I split up his---and Twig's---clothes, armor, weapons, and pack. We were heavily burdened now. With any luck, not for very long.

Twig stood up. She walked up to Centaur and rubbed her head against him. She turned and trotted up the trail. Centaur followed her.

We began heading in the same direction a couple of minutes later. We wanted to give them a head start, but not too much. They were traveling faster than us. If events proceeded as planned, the trail would be safe once we reached where the monkeys had held it hostage. It took longer than anticipated. How far away could Twig smell? Our pace quickened as we began to hear rustling in the trees and loud chirps. If the monkeys got frustrated chasing the wolves, they would likely return to where they ambushed unsuspecting travelers. To our left, away from the river, a dozen pale-brown monkeys swung through the trees. They hooted and howled as they tried to keep up with the two wolves. They were traveling parallel to the trail, but westbound. The monkeys were the size of the wolves, with claws extended from all four paws. It definitely would have been a challenge to fight so many of them with just the five of us. The two wolves' mouths were open widely, with their tongues hanging out---a display of canine bliss. For some couples, a dinner and a movie was a great date. For these two, sending a dozen carnivorous monkeys on a goose chase couldn't be beat.

We had traveled another two kays by the time the wolves returned to us. They followed us for another two, sniffing closely behind us, before they returned to their human forms. They were laughing so hard they had trouble dressing. Centaur stopped, a pained look on his face.

We became concerned, Hornet on the verge of panic. "You're not dying from the change, are you?"

"I think I strained a muscle from laughing so hard. You should have seen those stupid monkeys trying to keep up. Some of them actually fell out of the trees."

Suddenly serious, Twig said, "I think we need to limit how often we change, especially before we enter a hazardous area. We both survived *this* change, but we may not always be so lucky. When we're not properly rested, stresses magnify. Injuries shock our system, becoming far more likely to be fatal."

"Agreed."

The difficulty with rough terrain wasn't just the extra effort we had to give to traverse it, it also took longer to pass through it. If the Trail of Dread was relatively flat and straight, we may have reached Ling-Ching by the end of the second day. The sun began to dim with two-thirds of our journey remaining.

An hour after reuniting with Centaur and Twig, the incline became severe and the vegetation stunted. The prickly, tree laden hills became smooth pastoral knolls. Animals ate heartily from the lush, open grasses. Herds of deer and sheep meandered from one elevated meadow to another.

"We need to camp away from the road," I suggested. "In the Negative Frontier, the prescience of other people doesn't always mean safety."

We searched for a good camp site, heading south, away

from the Amber River. Water was as much as an attractor for animals, and monsters, as gold was for humans. It was easy to hide once away from the road. The hills created a natural barrier. Two-hundred meters from the Trail of Dread was sufficient. As long as we kept voices to a whisper, and didn't have a campfire, no one would know we were there.

"As a precaution, Centaur and I will alternate in canine form," said Twig. "If something approaches, we'll be able to smell them in advance of them invading our camp. No, dear, we can't run together tonight. Two hours each as a wolf will allow us to change form tomorrow, if needed."

With Centaur and Twig providing the watch, I permitted myself a full night's sleep. A rarity on the road. But being so accustomed to minimal sleep, I wasn't able to sleep the entire night. I woke an hour before dawn. I remained prone, listening to the night sounds. It was Twig's watch. As she listened and sniffed, her paws rested on Centaur's chest. Periodically, she would patrol the perimeter of the camp. After concluding everything was fine, she would return to her mate.

I couldn't stand it any longer. I had to get up. I greeted Twig, then departed camp to take a night stroll. She growled quietly at me.

"I know, I shouldn't be going off alone at night," I whispered to her, "but I can't lay here either. I'll be careful, and I won't go far."

I took my bow with me, more precaution than prediction. With the terrain being free of floral obstacles, and my eyesight being as good as it was, I was confident I wouldn't be taken by surprise. My one reservation was something coming quickly around one of the hills. My hearing, although not as good as my sight, was still better than a human's. Even if I didn't see the thing coming, I would be able to hear it---I hoped.

A herd of sheep slept two knolls over. It amazed me no one had taken advantage of the clustered meat. Many people were vegetarian on Limbo, due to not knowing if what one caught was once one's friend. Those in the Negative Frontier ignored such taboos. The sheep were probably too far from the Amber River. Definitely too far from Ling-Ching, the Dreadful Mountains' sole significant settlement.

I must have fallen asleep watching the sheep, because what I saw carry one of them away could only be found in a dream. It was a giant eagle, with a four-meter wingspan. But that wasn't what was most amazing. Instead of having a bird's head it had the bust of a stag. It had a full rack, its razor-sharp antlers glistening in the moon light. The sheep it carried was small, only a lamb. It baaed incessantly, waking its brethren below. Humans weren't permitted to reproduce on Limbo, but there was a necessity for animals to do so if the ecosystem was to sustain itself. If an adult was taken I may have allowed it to escape, but it had taken a baby.

I aimed for the top of one of its wings, where bones, muscles, and tendons met. I heard a snap. The stag screeched painfully, then dived in the direction of the wing I clipped. To attempt a re-ascent the creature released its prey. I should have known that injuring the stag would kill the lamb as effectively as eating it. I couldn't watch as the lamb hit the rolling grass with a padded thud.

The cries and commotion woke up more than the sheep. An evenly paced thumping echoed through the hills as the ground shook around me. The sound was getting louder, indicating what was making the sound was approaching.

"WHY?!!!" billowed over the hills, before dampening in swirling eddies in the clefts between them. The creature was immense. It stood five meters, from leathery toes to matted thatch: Lord Dung. He was one of the four gents that lived in Chaneg. Did having the largest contingency of gents mean that being Chaotically Negative was the norm for a gent? If gents weren't exposed to outside influences would we all become Chaotically Negative? Had I already become one of them? Was I re-created on the Chaotic-Negative side of the tracks instead of Neutrality?

Lord Dung looked down at the broken lamb, and the stag. "Why do these things always happen to me?" The gent had experienced a series of unfortunate events, from the moment he arrived on Limbo. When he walked through the portal that transported him to Limbo, the first thing he stepped on was a pile of animal feces. As he cleaned his feet in the grass a buffalo gored him from behind. He had preferred to be called *Gore*, a more fitting name for a gent. Instead, the person who first met him chose *Dung*, a derivative of the last word he uttered. Lord Dung's road to the Chaotic-Negative Frontier was a short one.

He became enraged. He pried the stag from the top of the lamb, where the two had gruesomely melded upon impact. He threw it as far as he could. It struck one of the sheep, knocking it into the next. Ten of the creatures were bowled over. "NO!!!" He ran towards the fallen animals. Those not injured ran away. Those directly hit didn't move at all. The two less injured, did, but with much anguish. Lord Dung raised his fists into the air and bellowed.

I thought it best not to have any contact with my brother. I returned to camp as slyly as I could. I wasn't surprised to find my friends awake and preparing for battle. "It's time to break camp. One of my brothers is having a particular bad day, and if he discovers us the day may not go so well for you either."

I explained what had occurred as succinctly as possible. The sooner I told the tale the sooner the shame of sharing an association and race with Lord Dung would begin to fade.

Chapter 22

SUMAC

Be it the lack of unchanged, or the propensity for isolation and solitude, there was only one settlement of substantial size in the Dreadful Mountains. The other habitations consisted of small clusters of people who harvested from a particular mine. These dozen or so hamlets had as many mutants living in them as unchanged. The haphazard compilation of shacks and mansions, industrial and commercial edifices, and venues of ill-repute that comprised Ling-Ching clung to the headwaters of the Amber River, where rolling hills transitioned into craggy peaks.

As we entered the village we nearly got run over by the barrage of oxen being unhitched and barges loaded. The Dreadful Mountains economy consisted of a four-part chain. First, there were the people who mined the oar and harvested the stone slabs. Then, there were the people who bought them, those working in the Clearinghouse. Third, were the short-shore-men, the people who loaded the precious minerals and building supplies onto the barges. Finally, there were the haulers, the people who floated down the river, escorted the oxen back to Amber, and pulled the barges upstream. The middlemen made the most money, those working in the Clearinghouse. They rarely touched the products, but they profited the most from them. Second in the pecking order were the short-shore-men. They worked for the Clearinghouse. In addition to loading barges, they provided security for the operation. They were indiscriminate in their discipline. As many miners and haulers were harmed or killed as highwaymen.

A separate, but related segment of the economy, was the row of pubs that were beneficial in lessening the weight of coins the miners, haulers, and short-shore-men, carried. The alcohol, food, and women were cheap, in quality, but not necessarily in price. The only alternative was supplying them themselves or getting their fill in Amber.

Before entering the village, we had connected the spheres together to better approximate the location of the fifth. As feared, it was far into the mountains. There were three roads leading away from Ling-Ching. The one we arrived on that paralleled the river. A road that led north, along the crest of the Troll Hills. And the continuation of the Trail of Dread, a north-easterly route that traversed the heart of the Dreadful Mountains. The latter was allegedly very steep and narrow at times, navigating five passes. It ultimately transitioned into the northern route, becoming a loop. The road was primarily used by miners, providing them partial access to their mines. The only other people who traversed it were men in a bad mood, who wanted to kill or be killed, and those seeking treasure, either from the miners or other things that hoarded precious minerals or gems. Wild men living in the mountains, some human, others not so much anymore, often raided the mines and hamlets. Their accumulated wealth rivaled the Clearinghouse's.

Twig joining our group had unexpected detriments. The scarcity of women on Limbo made them more noticeable. Working weeks in a mine with just men beside you amplified the attraction. The looks the men gave Twig weren't meant for a woman they intended to take home to mom.

Centaur was particularly concerned. "The less time we spend here the better."

"We're going to need to hire a guide," Hornet proposed. "Unless you think the sphere is just sitting beside the road somewhere. The Dreadful Mountains have hundreds of peaks. We're just as likely to die from starvation after getting lost as we are from attack."

"Is there anyone here we can trust?" asked General Paint.

"No," said Twig, "but I don't think we have another choice. I'm good at tracking people, not objects."

"Where do you think we can find such a person?" I asked. "Looks like everyone is busy doing something."

"I know just the place," said Centaur. We followed him to the *Fool's Abode*, the most run-down tavern in Ling-Ching. "Anyone who is that down and out to be willing to be hired by us would have to reside in a place like this."

Reside wasn't a metaphor. There were people actually huddled against the walls of the tavern on beer-soaked bedrolls. It was remarkable they were able to sleep with the racket the upright patrons were making.

"Maybe they're dead," Hornet suggested.

"That would explain the smell." Twig covered her nose and mouth. She wasn't easily offended by odors. Spending most of her life outdoors she was exposed to many horrific---and wonderful---smells. But earthy odors, like musk or rot, weren't the same as stale human smells.

Most of the men looked emaciated, like they hadn't eaten anything substantial in weeks. The only man who looked healthy enough to survive a few days in the wilderness wasn't really a man. He was about a head taller than a human, slightly shorter than me. He appeared to be one of those wild men we heard about. He was mainly human, but there was a bit of animal in him too. He looked pre-historic, but with less attractive features.

Centaur shook the man with his boot, circumventing the insanitariness of touching him with his hand. The man grunted, then flipped over on his other side. He put his thumb in his mouth and went back to sleep.

"It looks like he was never weaned," Twig scrutinized. "Bet he's a momma's boy."

"You're the closest thing we have to his mother," stated

General Paint. "Not all wars are won on the front line."

Twig looked disgusted, but the sooner she was out of this town the better. In the sweetest voice she could muster she said, "Time to get up."

The primitive man's jaw clenched. I thought he might completely bite through his thumb. He released it, revealing teeth marks chiseled deeply into it. He turned away from the voice, covering his head with his arms.

"Mama's going to be upset if you don't get up. I've fixed you breakfast."

I don't know if it was the threat or the food, but he turned towards Twig, opening one eye. "Yu don luk like mee mama. Mee mama wus fat un uglee. Yu pritee laydee."

"Breakfast will be ready in a minute." Twig directed her mate, with a hand motion, to procure the food. Centaur obediently walked up to the tavern keep. The primitive man leaned up on his elbows. He appeared to have trouble focusing. His bloodshot eyes squinted. The dim light in the tavern was too much for him. He shut his eyes, but remained propped. His clothes were skins, but tailored to fit him. He wore a tunic, trousers, and boots. The latter had wooden soles.

He opened his eyes again when he smelled a platter of spiced meat, and a steaming bowl of porridge. Centaur set them beside the man. He returned a moment later with a mug of a purplish liquid and a crudely made metal spoon. The man bypassed the utensil, alternately dipping his fingers into the porridge and licking them with stuffing his mouth with the meat. The state his hands were in, half the food's flavor was from what had been on them previously. He took a sip of the beverage. He immediately spit it out.

"Tays fonee."

"That's because it doesn't have alcohol in it," said Centaur. "Wilderberry juice has vitamins. You don't want to end up like them." Centaur pointed to men lying on the floor in worse shape---

substantially worse shape---than the primitive man. "Days away from being re-created."

"Thay oglee. Thay week."

"If you want to *stay* big and strong, you need to drink it," said Twig.

With the sourest of expressions, like he was imbibing the nastiest tasting medicine ever created, the primitive man emptied his mug. He shivered when he was finished.

"I'm Twig. This is Centaur, Hornet, General Paint, and Pulp."

"Yu Ohger?"

"I'm a gent. I live more than a thousand kays from here, in the Copper Forest."

"I wish eye liv dow send kays away en copperd forst."

"Maybe you will, one day," said Centaur.

"Will you tak mee to copperd forst?"

"If I'm his momma, that makes you his daddy."

"If you help us find something in the mountains I'll take you to the Copper Forest with me one day."

The primitive man stood up. "Let's go." Porridge covered his mouth.

Twig borrowed a washcloth from the tavern keep and washed his face. The proximity to him was too much. She had to back away. "What's your name?"

"I Su-mac."

"Well Sumac. Before we do anything else you need to bathe."

"Yu wash mouf."

"There are other things on a body that need to be washed." Sumac began to undress. Twig stopped him mid-disrobe. "No, I'm not going to wash you. A tub of water will."

"No lik wadder."

"That's obvious."

"It cold. Skin skratch afder."

"You will like a hot bath." Twig motioned for Centaur to

make the arrangements.

He returned with a frown. "The Fool's Abode doesn't have any hot water or tubs, but there's an inn by the Clearinghouse that does."

"If the place is decent maybe we all can take a bath. Before you make an excuse that we don't need to spend money on something as frivolous as a bath, remember you now have a mate. Women like hot baths, even women who spend most of their time outdoors."

"Maybe just you can take a bath then."

"And men who bathe regularly are more likely to have women snug up against them."

"You didn't care so much about being clean when we were wolves."

"If you only want to be close to wolves, don't bathe, but we're not in wolf form now, are we? Sometimes being next to a woman is nicer than being next to a wolf."

With hot, clean water being such a luxury, baths were not cheap. To save money, we recycled tub water. Twig, of course, was first. She wanted Sumac to go next. We informed her what the water might look like after he got done. She definitely didn't want Centaur in that.

The water had cooled off by the time Sumac hesitantly got in, but it was still much warmer than he was used to. Sumac couldn't just sit there and let the grime loosen up. He had to play. He splashed around like he was a toddler. The bathhouse was soaked, as were those who supervised him.

Twig came in 10 minutes later. "He doesn't look very clean. One of you is going to have to scrub him." Twig left again.

"I guess I better do it," said Centaur. "Was Dinga ever this bossy?"

"No, but Twig has had more practice. I fear what my life will be like when the two women meet."

"Maybe they won't like one another?"

"Even if they don't, women in close proximity will talk."

"Weren't you in a long-term relationship, Pulp?"

"And it drove me to join you on this quest."

"There has to be something good about having a wife," stated General Paint. "If I ever retire I thought I might settle down with one. I wouldn't mind someone taking care of me."

"They'll take care of you, all right, but in their own way."

"A trog would never allow himself to be henpecked."

Twig took that moment to walk in, to check on the progress of scrubbing down Sumac. We got very quiet. She raised an eyebrow. She looked past Centaur, who was drenched in water, to Sumac. "He looks much better. You enjoy taking a hot bath, Sumac?"

"I like buppels. I don thin yu luk lik hen."

"Who says I look like a hen?" Sumac turned towards us. Twig smirked as she followed his eyes, particularly when they fell on Centaur. "Well, hens don't like to get romantic, even with people who take hot baths." Twig walked out of the bath house again, this time humming.

"Now look at what you did," said Centaur. "I took a bath for nothing."

We got two rooms in the inn. We spent most of what remained of our money, but considering it might be another week before we slept in a bed---if we were lucky---Twig declared it was worth it. Centaur may have been threatened, but he did end up sharing a room with his mate. From the activity in their room they didn't get much sleep. Sumac was not used to sleeping on a bed, making it difficult for him to fall asleep. He rolled around a lot---next to me. He finally fell asleep after falling on the floor. He snored terribly, but that was better than getting elbowed every couple of minutes.

Chapter 23

MINERS

We had two problems. First, we didn't know---exactly---where the next sphere was. Access to the first four was direct. Down this road. Head in that direction. It was never easy procuring them, but we always found them. Travel in the Dreadful Mountains was difficult enough following a road. The sphere wasn't going to be beside a road. Maybe not even at the end of a game trail. It was out there somewhere, to the east. Being so close to the boundary shield, that meant less than a hundred kays. Two days on a sparse plain or a road. Weeks perhaps in the mountains. Endless climbs and descents. Dead-end canyons. A second problem, the sphere wasn't stationary. All the spheres had to have moved at one time or another for them to be so dispersed, but this one was still moving.

"Are you sure about that?" asked Centaur.

"I can't be certain about anything on Limbo," Hornet replied. "There are subtle changes in the pull and direction."

"We're going to need help."

"Sumac will help us, won't you?" spoke Twig.

"Su-mac help. Su-mac tak yu tu minurs."

"Let's hope the miners are as helpful," said Centaur.

"The Lich spoke of one of the spheres being with the trolls," I said. "This is troll country."

"You're assuming he spoke the truth," General Paint responded.

"Why would he lie? He was going to kill us."

"Those living in this frontier have schemes upon schemes," said Twig. "You apparently defeated this lich, because you are here. What if he allowed himself to be killed, as a rouse to disseminate erroneous information."

"He did mention us helping him by collecting the two spheres he couldn't himself, those in the Positive Frontier," said Hornet. "Maybe we're helping him *more* by collecting all six spheres."

"We must take advantage of this information, be it honest or subversive," said Centaur. "We might get a better response with *Where are the trolls?* than *Where is the sphere?*"

The first mining hamlet we came to was populated---predominantly---by people that looked like Sumac. They didn't welcome us, but they didn't attack us either. Our guide helped tremendously. With concentration we were able to pick out a few words, but not enough to piece together the conversation. There was more laughing than talking.

Sumac explained. "Thay tink yu dum fur nut no-in trolls no liv her. Ogur camp closer."

"I thought you were an ogre," said Hornet.

"No ogur. I ogra. Oger biggur."

The next hamlet Sumac led us to was predominantly ogre. The creatures were about my height. They wore clothes, but just barely. The hides that covered them were not properly tanned. Bits of decayed flesh was still attached to them. They reeked worse than the black drak's musk. They looked more animal-like, more feral, than Sumac's people. No words were recognizable this time.

They were agitated we were in their camp, they likely assuming we were there to take their ore. In the center of camp was a fire pit. On a metal grate above coals, meat roasted. Everything imaginable---and some things that weren't---was being cooked. A pile of scraps, predominantly bones, was beside the fire ring.

"Is that a human skull?" asked Hornet.

"Meat is meat," stated Twig.

"You haven't eaten any...humans, have you?"

"Gaea, no. But I have eaten mutes while in canine form. Like I said, meat is meat. A wolf needs to eat. A kill mustn't be permitted to spoil. On Limbo we are blatantly aware that flesh is just what shrouds our soul. Every few years our shrouds change."

General Paint appeared perturbed.

"No, I haven't eaten any trogs," Twig assured him. "Or gents. I've only eaten those things that have a passing resemblance to humans. And only those I have killed. I'm not a scavenger."

Time to change the subject. Centaur turned to our guide. "Do they know where the trolls are?"

"Thay no lik trolls. Trolls no di. Trolls no fite fair. Thay no know were trolls go. Thay choos no kil yu. Thay lik gints."

"About time that someone does," I muttered. The ogres were staring at me. They appeared to be in awe, as if someone famous, a celebrity, was in their midst. Why were there so few gents, but so many other things my size? Was a singular mutation rarer than multiple mutations? When did a person who mutated in size, mutate sufficiently in other ways for them to no longer be considered human enough to be called a gent? My appearance was more mutated than most gents. My ears were like an arbol's. My teeth, like an equine's. I had gills like a mer. If I mutated anymore, would I no longer be able to retain my membership in the Brotherhood?

"Let's leave while they still feel that way about you, Pulp," said Centaur. "Fighting a dozen ogres is more of a challenge than we want right now."

"Or ever," Hornet quietly added.

The next hamlet we came to was an even mix of human and ogra. Why were some people attracted to their own kind and others to those who were different? Being in the Chaotic Frontier I would have assumed most of the humanoids here would prefer variety. It was a pleasant change to be able to communicate without translation.

"Trolls don't come this far down," spoke the leader of the camp. We looked up, into the mountains. The top third of them were covered in snow, with intermittent glaciers down twice that far.

"How far down do they go?" asked Centaur.

"About halfway. They used to live farther down, into the hills even, but with the explosion of population they fled. They like a good man-steak now and then, but they don't like to fight so hard for it. Their wounds regenerate, but it still takes a while to complete one of their hunts if they are consistently hacked at. You wouldn't enjoy being in a swarm of mosquitoes, but you would triumph in the end. You wouldn't want to join our crew for a month or two, would you? Having a gent and a trog would make up for those who have fled for potentially more productive mines."

"Do the mines further up into the mountains really have higher grade ore?" asked General Paint.

"Not that I've heard. I think most leave for the thrill of the latest and newest. Everything is better on the other side of the mountain, or up the next slope."

"Thank you for the offer," said Centaur. "But it's urgent we find the trolls. They have something we need."

"Never met someone so anxious to be mutated. I hope it's worth it to you, like I hope it's worth it to those who have fled the lower mines for the upper ones. In exchange for mining a predictable amount, and quality, of ore and stone, there aren't as many things trying to kill us. It may be boring, but much safer. One of the reasons troll stay up there is their food supply following them. If you return not too mutated the offer stands about helping us with this mine."

We wished him well, then headed further up into the mountains. There wasn't anything close to resembling a road up there, but there were paths. The three hamlets we had visited so far had all been adjacent to the Trail of Dread. Leaving the last true connection to civilization reinforced how dangerous the next few days might be.

Lord Tick, my least lofty brother, controlled the first upper camp we came to. He was insecure about his height, and it showed. Physically he was no taller than Sumac, but the platform shoes he wore raised him another 30 sims. He also wore a hide top hat, that added another 40 sims. His companions were all human. All were below average in height, making him appear even taller.

He was not happy when he saw me. "This is my kingdom, Pulp. You return to the Copper Forest, or the Western Sea, wherever it is you dawdle."

"We'll be happy to leave as soon as you answer some questions," said Centaur.

"You will not address me unless first spoken to." Lord Tick's face was beginning to turn red.

"Be civil, to retain some dignity," I said to him. "Centaur is nearly your height, weighs as much as you, and is probably stronger. We're looking for trolls."

"Trolls are forbidden in my realm. What's *he* doing here?" Lord Tick looked like he was having a bowel movement as he studied Sumac. "His kind is also forbidden."

"Yu no luk lik gint."

Lord Tick face continued to darken. His breathing became more intense. He looked like a percolating tea kettle on the verge of whistling. The skin below his right eye begun to pulse. He detached the irregular piece of iron sticking out of his hide belt. From a distance it may have resembled a sword.

"We'll be leaving now," I said. "Any violence on your part will not end well for you. Next time the Brotherhood meets they'll get a good laugh at how easily you were defeated."

We immediately left the camp. Sure, we would have been able to defeat Lord Tick and his associates, but there was the possibility of one of us dying. Best case scenario, most of us would be bruised and mildly injured. Hardly the state we wished to be in when we confronted the trolls.

"One would think with having this so-called *Brotherhood* you gents would get along better," said Hornet. "It's not much of an alliance, is it?"

"If the need was great enough, I'm confident we would come together. Maybe not all of us, but enough to make a difference. Great power does breed great egos. Drak have enough sense to not pretend to be united."

"The Brotherhood must try," Twig insisted. "Communication remedies some problems, and prevents others. I've spent a significant portion of my life as an animal that takes comfort from the pack. I might be a bit biased in my views."

"You look amused," Centaur commented after noticing me smirking.

"Just remembering Thumbringer defeating Lord Tick at Cloud Home. You remember Thumbringer?"

"One of Dinga's companions, before she joined us. That must have been embarrassing for him. Devastating in front of his peers?"

"Prior to our assembly, Lord Tick spent some time in Capetown, to torment the local inhabitants, to boost his ego."

"Karma," Hornet stated.

"Gaea," Twig countered. "Payback occurs after we die on Limbo. While living, it's all up to us."

The next camp we came to had a true mix living in it. There were humans, ogra and ogres. It was the largest of the hamlets we had visited. More than a score worked in the mine. They were civil---so far. The sun was beginning to dim. They generously shared their settlement with us. They fed us. They even offered to give up their beds, so we might have a soft place to sleep. We accepted the board. A large stack of ore was piled outside the mine, larger than we had seen in the other camps, even in relation to the number of workers they had.

The mayor of the co-operative was named Marmot. He was an ogra, but a very intelligent one. What he lacked in intelligence he made up in organization and leadership. He was not only well-liked by his men, but respected. It was remarkable he was re-created in the Chaotic-Negative Frontier. He either had changed significantly since then, or had done something so Chaotic and so Negative to transcend his Positive-Order tendencies.

"This is the life, isn't it?" he said to us beside the large bonfire that lit up not only the camp, but the mountainside beside it. "Fresh air. A good view. Relaxing after a hard day's work."

"It must get boring doing the same thing every day---and tiring," commented Centaur.

"Every vein of silver or gold is unique. How can stretching one's muscles be boring? Not doing anything all day, now that's boring. The repetition of the pick is soothing. The more complicated my labors the less I can daydream? A perpetual paid vacation."

"I don't think anyone has described mining in quite that way before," said General Paint.

"It's all attitude. You can choose to be happy in what you do, or not."

A camp was most vulnerable at dawn. Not only are people more tired at the end of a watch, they become more complacent.

There are two kinds of people. Those who become successful from their own merit. And those who ride the coattails of others. Those that produce something. And those who don't. Mining is hard work, but sometimes, extremely profitable. If the hard work could be circumvented, all the better.

No one was expecting the raid, including us. Why wouldn't a hamlet this size be safe? We assumed whatever precautions had to be taken would be. The creatures that tore through camp looked similar to those whose camp they plundered. They were a mix of ogre, ogra, and human. Their clothing was in better shape than the clothing of the people they stole from. They carried bludgeons instead of blades. Their intention was to incapacitate, not to kill. Dead people couldn't produce more ore or purchase more supplies. With the precision only much practice produced, the marauders took the most valuable goods and fled. None of the gold ore remained. And only half of the food. Other things were taken, including the best articles of clothing, but overall the camp was permitted to sustain itself until it was restocked. Before our wits were freed from their slumber, the marauders were already heading higher into the mountains.

We attempted to chase them down, but were forced back when boulders were thrown down at us. Two of the miners were killed when one of the rocks landed on one of them and rolled over the other. The two bodies were stripped of their clothing and tossed further down the mountains. In an ogre majority camp, they may have been eaten. The half-dozen in the hamlet suppressed their urges to appease the sensibilities of the majority.

The miners looked more downtrodden than angry. Even Marmot's enthusiasm was drained a bit. "May Gaea re-create Hedgehog and Salmon as she feels fit. That was a month's worth of ore. I guess we'll have to work harder the next couple of months to make up for it."

"Aren't you even a bit upset about them stealing your ore?" I asked.

"What's done is done. The raiders won't come back for three more months. Life is cyclical. This is our low."

"If you knew the raiders were coming, why didn't you prepare for them?" asked Hornet.

"We do, to some degree. When it's time for them to hit our camp, we reduce our stock. Of course, our prediction of their arrival is approximate. Sometimes we guess better and have practically nothing for them to take. Other times we have piles of ore, like we had today."

"Couldn't you just hide your most valuable things?" asked

Centaur.

"If we don't have anything for them to take, why do we exist? That's what the raiders would think. They'll use swords next time instead of clubs, and all 23 of us---now 21---would perish instead of just two."

"Do you belittle existence that much that two dying is insignificant?" asked Twig.

"We cherish life in this camp, but we understand that these shells that surround our souls aren't eternal. Everyone dies. Everyone is re-created."

"You were a member of the Third Time Is A Charm Church, weren't you?" asked Centaur.

"I was a Third Timer before I realized making love to Gaea was less enlightening than making love to Gaea's world."

General Paint huddled us. "This camp must be under the same moral influence as Trogdom, but in reverse."

"Positivity is leaking into their mine?" Hornet speculated.

"Sounds innocuous, but are good intentions enough?" Centaur questioned. "Passiveness may postpone violence, or even limit it, but it rarely extinguishes it."

"Maybe they are just content with their lifestyle," I conjectured. "They appear happy."

"Allowing themselves to become cattle is repugnant," said Centaur. "They may not be eaten like cattle, but they are beasts of burden."

"Are you saying that Gaea is tampering with people beyond re-creating them?" Twig questioned.

"I don't think Gaea is intentionally doing it," I said. "Precious minerals are clustered in veins. Maybe morality is, too. Limbo is causing us to constantly change, not just physically, but intellectually, and emotionally."

"What would happen if someone who was already Negatively-Chaotic hit a Negative-Chaotic pocket?" Centaur asked.

"Let's hope that never happens," said Twig.

"Eye hun-gree," said Sumac.

"We all are, dear, but I don't think these people can afford to give us more food."

We were wrong. "Please join us for breakfast before you leave. And take some extra for your travels."

The food smelled great. The shock of the raid appeared to be completely over for the miners. They were smiling and laughing, having a grand old time in each other's company. Marmot placed a bowl of food in front of each of us. It was strips of meat cooked with some sort of root. "Please eat. We don't know what the day has in store for us. If we die today how will conserving food change that?" He had a point.

We ate what was offered, thanking Marmot and his crew profusely. We would have given them a portion of our own in return if we knew how long we would be in the mountains. We had been more cautious in safeguarding our supplies. Nothing of ours was taken.

"Return whenever you like," spoke Marmot, down slope from us. "There's always work and a home for you here." We smiled politely at him, then continued our ascent. It sounded inviting. Was it worth the occasional raiding injury and loss of property to be in a perpetual blissful stupor? Many would jump at the opportunity.

Chapter 24

WHITE

We pinpointed the location of the sphere again. We were getting closer. It was higher in the mountains---and still moving. What were the trolls doing with it?

Sumac took us to two more hamlets, each bringing us closer to the snow line. Consistent replies to our queries were *Why do you want to find them?* and *They are higher up*. When asked about the raiders, the miners displayed their injuries---all valiantly received---an indication they were more hesitant in allowing the rewards of their hard work to leave them. The raiders were also said to be *higher up*. Occasionally, an attempt was made to raid the raiders, but none were successful. The raiders supposedly lived in a cave complex---no one had actually seen it. Their leader was a man five meters tall. He wore hides like most of his crew. Instead of carrying a club, he carried a sling. His projectiles may have looked like pebbles, in proportion to his height, but they were over ten sims in diameter. It was rare for someone to be hit by one and live. He also threw boulders, but they were too large to carry. The few he hurled he found on site.

"That sounds like Lord Thump," I said. "He likes to hit things. Anything that moves is fair game. A bird. A rabbit. Fish. People. A tree on a windy day. He's more cautious now. A few years ago he killed one of Lord Nettle's servants. We had to hold both of them back. A gent striking another gent is automatic expulsion."

"Haven't most of the Negative gents we've encountered

tried to kill you?" asked Hornet.

"Not directly. A gent can't attack another gent. What his henchmen do, that's another story."

"I'm almost tempted to challenge this Lord Thump," said Centaur.

"Except we have a mission to accomplish," Twig reminded him. "Women are supposed to be the ones who go around in circles, who are easily distracted, but anytime something comes along to challenge a man, be it another man, an animal, a tree or a stream, he goes off on a tangent to confront it."

"The problem is that men come with a built-in pointer," I commented. "It doesn't always point in the wisest direction."

"No mor up," stated Sumac.

"So, there aren't any more camps higher up?" Centaur questioned.

"No mor."

"Do you think you can track the trolls, Twig?"

"I can track anything if I first get a good sniff of it. You wouldn't have any troll urine on you?"

"There is someone who might be able to help us," I said. "Thump and Tick aren't the only gents living in the Dreadful Mountains. Lord Bruin lives in an ice castle on one of the highest peaks. He named his residence after the mountain it was built on: *Ursa Major*."

"He's not going to be one of those gents that allow their violence do the talking for him?" asked Centaur.

"Lord Bruin is the least brutish of the Negative gents. Some might even call him *civilized*. In comparison to his brethren, he is downright refined."

"And he will be happy to help us?" asked Twig.

"He is very political. He would sell his mother if it might benefit him down the road."

"Don't sell your soul," cautioned General Paint.

"My soul has been in flux since I arrived on Limbo. I don't

think a bit of fine-tuning will hurt it much."

There wasn't a trail that led to Ursa Major, so we had to bushwhack, first on scree, then on snow. I knew, approximately, where the ice castle was. I had transported there using the platform I kept near the arbols in the Copper Forest. Looking down looked much different than looking up.

Sumac's help was no longer needed, but he continued to follow us, like a family pet. I felt sorry for him, but seeing him smiling I reconsidered. Walking in the mountains, with its fresh air and its great views, had to be better than sleeping it off on the floor of a pub. His prescience wasn't a burden. His good nature was the glue that kept us emotionally sound. I also felt he still had something to contribute. I just didn't know what that contribution might be.

There were only so many things we could carry, and snow gear wasn't one of them. Our feet not only got cold and wet, they tended to slip---a lot. Fearing a tumble down the mountain, we roped together. If one of us slipped, the majority of us would---likely---retain our footing. Worst case scenario was a chain-reaction fall. At least we would die together, what companionship was all about.

The cold wasn't too bad, as long as we kept moving. Not just warm, but sweating from the exertion. Whenever we took a break the moisture on my skin would immediately cool me. Whenever I remained inactive for more than a few minutes I would become chilled to the bone. And when the wind blew, which it frequently did when climbing a mountain, it blew through you, like you weren't wearing clothes, or skin. Ten to twenty kay per hour bursts were palatable. When they reached forty or fifty it felt like icy shards were stabbing me.

The only person who appeared content was Sumac. This was an adventure for him. Not a chore. He grinned like he was a yearling, which wasn't too far from his intellectual age. Crunching through snow, with an end of the world view---quite literally, we were that close to the opaque boundary shield---was a significant upgrade to lying passed out on a smelly, sticky floor of a bar.

As wind picked up higher on the mountain, blowing snow reduced visibility to ten meters. My proficiency with a bow regulated me to an artillery position in our queue, but being the biggest and strongest I was placed in front. I had two jobs. Officially, as snowplow---what was knee-high to me came up to at least the chest of my companions. Unofficially, as locomotive---we were roped together and with me being in the lead I pulled them up the mountain.

"I can't see a thing," said Centaur. "If Twig and I were wolves...."

"We can't carry any more," Hornet insisted, "not with the snow and the incline."

Something frigid swooshed past me, striking General Paint, behind me. I believed it initially to be an avalanche, but an avalanche couldn't be that narrow in scope. Something pounced, then fled. The rope became slack behind me. I yanked on it, my intent, to pull the trog up from where he had fallen. The rope's frayed end slapped at me. "PAINT!"

"He's gone." Hornet had been tied to the other end of him. He displayed another piece of frayed rope.

"What was that?" asked Twig.

"I don't know," Centaur replied, "but I intend to find out. It's time we became wolves. Stay here as Twig and I find General Paint." That brief interlude between clothes and fur looked painful. There are parts of a man---and woman---that shouldn't be exposed to extreme temperatures.

The wolves ran off. It took them five minutes to return. Centaur changed back briefly to inform us what they had found. He wrapped his clothes around him as he barely got the words out of his quivering mouth. "If it wasn't for my canine sniffer I would never have found it. A drak, as white as the snow, has General Paint wedged in a hole atop a shelf. It blends in so perfectly that only movement, and my nose, betrayed it. The trog wasn't moving."

"Gen-Ral Pate ded?" The ogra questioned, appearing simultaneously confused and sad.

"Trogs are hearty folk."

"Do you think he's dead?" asked Hornet.

"He might be frozen," I replied, "in a state of suspended animation---elemental hibernation."

"Why not just kill him?"

"This drak may want to eat its food alive," said Centaur. "For some monsters it's more satisfying."

"Will the drak thaw him out first?" asked Hornet.

"A drak that lives in freezing temperatures probably prefers its food to be cold."

"Twig and I could distract him," Centaur suggested.

"I wouldn't recommend it," I said. "Those monkeys didn't have a breath weapon."

"Maybe there's some way to block the attack," Twig proposed.

"In wolf form?" Centaur questioned.

"There might be a way to distract the drac long enough---without someone getting hurt---to free General Paint," said Hornet. "Time to test the limits of this Grace of Gaea thing I supposedly have."

"You think this wise?"

"No, but I'm willing to try. Everyone else has been re-created. It might be my turn. How long do you think it will take to deplete the drak's discharge? After that we only have to contend with 25 sim long claws and teeth."

Hornet walked towards the drak. We paralleled his route, keeping our distance, so the drak would focus---solely---on his prescience. Centaur returned to wolf form. If something went wrong, he and Twig would initiate plan B. By then the drac may have exhausted its artillery.

The drak mustn't have been one of the brightest of its kind. It blew out a conical burst of cold air before Hornet was even in range. Concerned the drak may get frustrated from its impotency and discontinue its attack, Hornet got closer. The next attack had the distance, but it went astray. After the third unsuccessful strike, Hornet began walking away. The drak's rage escalated. It ran from the ledge towards its adversary.

Sumac and I darted to the trog as the two wolves stood guard. We carried General Paint's stiff body away.

From a distance we saw the drak miss with his breath attack at near point-blank range. The frost began as a concentrated ray, that terminated as a mist. It snapped at Hornet with its teeth, and swung at him with its claws. It was time for Centaur and Twig to join the skirmish. They bit at its tail. The creature, although 30 meters long, was agile. It spun around on its four legs. The two wolves rushed off. The drak, apparently forgetting its primary target, chased them. It ran at least as fast as a man, but not as fast as a wolf. Centaur and Twig didn't play fair. Not only did they slow down enough to give the drak some hope in catching them, they went up hill. After a couple of minutes, the drak collapsed, heaving.

"You think a drak ever died of a heart attack?" I asked Sumac. The ogra grinned.

Chapter 25

LORD BRUIN

We regrouped where Centaur and Twig had left their clothes and packs. They returned to human form, then dressed hastily, before the cold could find the crack it would use to relentlessly penetrate to their core. "I guessed right that things acclimated to the cold tire more easily when overheated," said Centaur. "And that the Grace of Gaea would protect you---even from a drak. How could it miss you that many times?"

Hornet smiled. "If it wasn't for your...belief...in me I may not have concurrently volunteered. It was more desperation, though, than faith---our only option if we had an option."

"I believe I saw General Paint's chest rise," I said.

Twig held his wrist. "He has a pulse too, but it's very faint, barely ten beats per minute."

"Let's see what we can do to thaw him out." Twig began to disrobe again.

"I find it simultaneously sentimental and disturbing, your desire to stimulate a friend," Centaur declared. "Not sure the effort is worth it, unconscious men enjoying such attention less than wake men."

"I'm not planning to become *that* intimate with him. To fully exploit the thermal dynamic properties of skin to skin contact, someone needs to strip off his clothes. Someone else bring me blankets. I'm not going to be able to help him if I'm as cold as he is." Twig and General Paint weren't completely naked, but close enough that *we* felt uncomfortable until they became buried beneath the covers.

The trog was first shocked, then terrified when he woke to find himself pressed tightly to a naked---nearly naked---woman. "No, stay next to me until you're completely thawed," she pleaded. "I don't plan on stripping in the cold any more today."

General Paint couldn't look at Twig. He focused on the horizon as the woman hugged him from behind. It took minutes for the embarrassment to build to an unbearable level. The trog withdrew from the covers and dressed. Twig chose to dress within the warmth of the blankets. Whenever I was in a particularly foul mood I thought back to them cuddling, General Paint with that pained look on his face.

We arrived at Ursa Major before it got dark, but just barely. Half-an-hour later, we would have had to camp out, the visibility at the periphery of the frontier, especially at night, making travel too hazardous.

The ice castle had perspired during the day, giving it a healthy glow, the liquid sheen creating a colorful kaleidoscopic spectacle. Ice sculptures greeted us on the entry plain. All were unique, of creatures exotic and familiar, animal and humanoid. Some of them were damaged, many of them unrecognizably.

Bi-pedal minks welcomed us. They were about General Paint's height. They wore a jeweled necklace, each unique, and a belt swollen with icy shards. The minks squeaked at us, then began walking towards the castle. In the manner they surrounded us they intended us to join them.

As the sun dimmed, the temperature dropped. Camping out tonight wouldn't have been pleasant.

On the ramparts, more of the minks watched. Icy shards, much larger than the ones the minks carried, were readied in ballistas. A drawbridge fell over the ravine that enveloped the castle.

We walked off the drawbridge onto the alcove between it

and eight-meter-tall double doors. A burst of warmth was felt as the doors opened outward. We were hurried in as the doors closed behind us.

The ice and cold of the exterior was forgotten once we stepped inside. Wood replaced frozen precipitation, in the form of beams, planks and paneling---and a roaring fire. The centralized four-sided fireplace percolated heat and ambiance throughout the 30-meter-tall great room. A stone chimney rose to the ceiling. A large pendulum clock hung from the center of it, the Limboan day slowly progressing. Clocks, although rare on Limbo, weren't absent. Instead of hours, there was moonlight and sunlight, each divided into three segments, further divided into four segments.

A stairway climbed to the ceiling, interrupted twice by the levels above us. I had been to Ursa Major before. The wonder remained, my admiration for the architecture and scenery perpetually refurbishing my awe.

A very tall man---Lord Bruin was a sim or two over five meters---looked down at us from the third story balcony. He was decked out in white fur, from boots to breeches, to coat, to hat. The fur looked like it had come from the minks. It had, but not sinisterly. Everyone dies. With the resources being so limited at this elevation, Lord Bruin preferred none of them to fallow.

"I feel chilled today." Lord Bruin's voice, like most gents, boomed. It ricocheted off the wood many times before it finally came to rest.

"To me it feels like I got a fever," said General Paint.

"Trogs are said to have stout constitutions." Lord Bruin squeaked something to the minks. They added a couple of logs to the fire.

"You could move to the tropics, brother," I suggested.

"There are too many people there. You're the first to visit me since Lord Coal two months ago. Now that's a hot natured fellow."

"I imagine he'll be more so the next time you see him. He

doesn't take defeat well."

"You were never one to shy away from your bigger brothers. You never initiated a fight, but you never backed away from one either. I've often wondered about that. It seems the smaller gents make up for their size in other ways. Does Gaea balance things out? Not entirely, because you are taller than your companions, unless they are more talented than you."

"My friends are quite talented. What's Thump up to? He has pissed off almost everyone in the Dreadful Mountains."

"Our kind hasn't been known to shy away from antagonism. Those with power are as likely to be infamous as famous. Thump wants to be King of the Mountains."

"Doesn't King Thump realize that stealing makes him look more petty than powerful. It makes all of us in the Brotherhood look bad."

"You should bring that up at the next meeting. Thump only associates terror with power. *Reputation* has too many syllables."

"I need your help."

"Obviously. I didn't think you climbed 4000 meters for exercise. I don't have anything in particular to trade for, but the Brotherhood is meeting next month. Something might come up. If not, it's beneficial to save a favor for a snowy day. Gaea, I hate a blizzard."

"The trolls have something we need. You wouldn't happen to know where they are holed up?"

"Which trolls? Trolls are even more numerous than gents in Chaneg."

"The trolls up here, of course. Did you think we went this far out of our way for discuss sea or desert trolls?"

Lord Bruin smiled wickedly. "How desperately do you need my help?"

"You sure you don't want to try courting Palm again? It might mellow her disposition."

"I don't like spiders. I'm no longer willing to exchange

potential gain for the unpleasantness that would follow." Lord Bruin eyed Sumac. "How about we trade straight up, for your servant."

"He's as much my companion as any of the others."

"Pity. I've decided to escort you to the trolls, personally. I need a cold shower, and nothing is much colder than stepping out my front door. The trolls are beginning to rough up the minken. Their migration from the multitude below has nearly brought them to my doorstep."

Chapter 26

FIRE AND ICE

When Lord Bruin volunteered to go he not only volunteered his assistance. Eight of the minken marched in front of us to the troll lair. In addition to the icy shards on their belts, they carried ammunition on the sash across their chests.

Load Bruin carried a platinum blade, as wide as a chain saw, and as long as I was tall. Beneath a white fur overcoat, he was ensconced head to toe in platinum armor, his helm embellished with ram horns.

My companions were initially shocked by his appearance, believing he had either stolen his gear from an Octagonal Knight, or had become one. A more detailed examination eased their concern. Envy, not larceny was the motivation for his attire. And preservation and efficiency---for someone not hindered by a budget.

Lord Bruin became a changed man once he stepped outside. He may have lived in a warm castle, but he toiled in a cold world. As we passed through the entry plain, Lord Bruin struck a large humanoid statue that could have been a troll. It shattered into a hundred pieces.

"Why destroy something so beautiful?" asked Twig.

"Beauty is fleeting. If I have control over it, I'm able to acquire it."

Hornet whispered to me, "Lord Bruin is eccentric, but I wouldn't classify him as Negative. Why is he in the Negative Frontier?"

"His romantic overtures aren't always of mutual consent. He prefers them not to be. He's controlling. Many of his encounters become violent. Some of his victims were young---more child than adult."

It took an hour to reach the troll lair. The creatures at the mouth of the cave may not have blended into the environment as flawlessly as their cousins in the hoodoos, but if one wasn't looking in the right direction they might be overlooked. They looked similar to the desert trolls, except their skin was white with a frosty blue tint.

Lord Bruin raised his gloved hand, then dropped it. Four of the minken threw icy shards at the trolls. Why perform such a futile act? If the trolls were part ice, how could they be harmed by ice? The impact of the shards was sufficient to shatter the limbs off the trolls, as proficiently as Lord Bruin shattered the ice sculpture. Their arms and legs began to regenerate, first as a bead of frozen precipitation at the stumps, that began to elongate. Two of the minken continued to throw icy shards at the two trolls. An equilibrium was reached. The trolls couldn't completely recover, but the minken couldn't completely destroy them either.

We didn't linger to see who would ultimately end the impasse. There were two more trolls a few steps within the cave. They were dispatched in a similar manner.

"Hold up," said Twig. She began to undress. Which gave Centaur permission to do likewise, he not wishing to be left behind. Lord Bruin's right eyebrow rose. Too cold for modesty, they bypassed token concealment as they changed into wolves.

A few more meters into the cave we began to hear voices---human ones. "Someone hasn't really joined up with the trolls, have they?" asked Centaur.

"Trolls like their food fresh," Lord Bruin elucidated. "Being lean, they prefer lean nourishment. They starve their captives before eating them."

We smelled the food pen before we saw it. The prisoners not eating didn't completely prevent them from defecated. One of the ogra fell into what could have been his own excrement. A troll on kitchen duty pulled him out. The humans, ogra, and ogres in the pen moved away from the food extraction, but slowly, the product of their fleeting energy reserves.

The next battle wasn't as strategic. It became a brawl. The minken threw their icy shards at the trolls from a distance as Lord Bruin charged them with his sword. He was a one-gent wrecking crew. He dispatched three of the creatures in the time it took the rest of us to dispatch one. The commotion drew the residual trolls into the kitchen. We were doing well, handedly winning the battle, but the trolls continued to regenerate, as we progressively tired.

Sumac may have been involved in a scuffle or two, but he was completely unprepared for so complex a battle. He stood bewildered as the rest of us fought. The captives had been deprived of food so long they were delirious. They no longer had someone guarding them, but they didn't have the sense to leave. Something paternal clicked in Sumac. He began herding the captives away from the melee. Not only was he assisting them in their freedom, he was also preventing any additional injuries or deaths. The holding pen was not designated as a safety zone. Some of the captives had been hit by incidental violence.

The battle persisted. Something had to be done. We hadn't

seen the sphere yet and we were becoming fatigued. We could free the captives, or find the sphere. We were too occupied to do both. We were able to counter the trolls' regenerative power twice. Could we do so a third time? What would permanently destroy ice? I looked down at one of the torches we carried into the cave. The trolls, seeing well in the dark, didn't require a light source, so we had to provide our own.

I threw the torch at one of the trolls. It made a pained expression as it melted where the torch had struck. The hole in the troll began to fill back in. The heat needs to be sustained. Short of shoving them into a volcano what could I do? We still had five elixirs. If only one of them could produce heat. I ran back to the entrance of the cave, where Centaur had dropped his pack as he disrobed. One of the vials had five bars on it. PURE RED ELEM!

I planned what I had to do before I swallowed the vial. I didn't want the trolls to regenerate when the heat expired, which meant the penta had to work as long as possible. If my friends did most of the damage all I had to do was keep the cavern warm enough that the trolls couldn't regenerate.

Here I go. I stepped as close to the center of the cavern as I safely could. I consumed the contents of the vial, then waited for the tingling sensation to begin. Electricity pulsed through my body. In a wide arc I swung my arms. I tried to release as little of the heat energy as possible. I perspired as the heat left my body from every direction, like the waves a pebble makes when it is dropped in a pool. With the added warmth, odors became more noticeable. The blood---and intestines, feces, and bile---became overwhelming. The heat appeared to be working. Through my stinging eyes I didn't see any of the trolls regenerating. I wanted to wipe my eyes, but any false movement might disrupt the discharge. With there being some warmth in the room now, the heat I needed to add, to maintain it, was minimal, which I was thankful for because the penta and I were almost expired. I no longer could see, but the sounds of battle remained, but were less intense. It reminded me of popcorn in a microwave. When the popping began to slow it was time to take it out. I collapsed. I should have felt the ground, but became unconscious before that happened.

Chapter 27

TALE

When I woke I was in Ursa Major, lying in a wooden four-post bed. Light shined through the glass pane in the middle of the log wall to my left. If I had to be re-created, this was definitely the way I wanted to return. A crystal goblet of water was on the night stand beside the bed. My throat felt like it was in a desert: gritty and parched. The door, to my left, was closed. It was deadly quiet. The room was either well-insulated or no one was around.

I pulled the minken comforter off me, then swung my legs onto the wood floor. I began to stand. Becoming dizzy, I allowed myself to fall back onto the bed. I took another sip of water, then restored the comforter. If I was going to be a convalescent, there were worse places to be.

The next time I woke, my friends were there, some sitting in chairs, others standing. Lord Bruin was also there, as was Sumac. “You’re awake,” spoke the master of the ice castle. “That’s a good sign. Is the bed comfortable enough for you?”

“Would me falling back to sleep in a couple of minutes be proof enough for you? I greatly appreciate you having a bed long enough for me. Most days it feels like I’m stumbling through a dollhouse."

"I have so few guests here I want them to be as comfortable as possible."

"Lord Bruin also has beds our size," Twig shared.

"And mine," General Paint added.

"Guests come in all sizes," Lord Bruin explained.

Sumac squeezed me through the covers. "Yu well?"

"I don't know about that, but I'm better."

"You did a good job of getting those people out of there."

"Thay git hert. Wee frends now. Wee start nu camp whur trolls."

"There's actually something there to mine?"

"There aren't any veins of gold or silver," stated General Paint, "but there are diamonds. I think Gaea was beginning to make this mountain a volcano, but changed her mind. Sumac and his new friends will be rich one day."

"If someone doesn't take the mine and diamonds away from them."

"They have squatter's rights," Lord Bruin declared. "Some of them have been in that cavern for weeks---against their free will---but they were still there. Around these parts spending a week in a place makes it yours. I'm giving Sumac and his crew sanctuary. If anyone bothers them they'll have to deal with me. That includes Lord Thump."

"Sumac wishes to share whatever profit he makes from the mine with us," said Centaur. "I couldn't disillusion the boy, so I told him it was a great decision, and we were very appreciative of the gesture. So, if everything goes well, we'll become rich too."

Sumac squeezed me again. "Frends help frends." Indeed they do, even friends who live in the Chaotic-Negative Frontier. Maybe it didn't matter if I was re-created on the wrong side of the boundary.

"This seems almost anti-climatic, but did you find the sphere?"

Hornet left the room for a moment and returned with a radiant orange orb.

"One to go, then. Tell me of your tale. Wasn't acquiring those spheres supposed to get progressively more difficult? It doesn't look like you came away with even a scratch. I was feeling guilty about not being able to help you after I became incapacitated. It looks like you didn't need it."

"Without your elemental outburst, we would never have been able to destroy the trolls," Centaur assured me. "The heat that almost killed you prevented the trolls from regenerating. Relying on their regeneration to sustain them, they never became proficient in fighting."

"It wasn't much of a battle," Lord Bruin agreed.

"So, after you dispatched the trolls, you found the orange sphere, and returned here?" I inquired.

"If some of the trolls didn't flee---with the sphere."

"I've never heard of trolls doing that."

"Apparently, some think with more than their incisors."

"So, you eventually caught up with these fleeing trolls, defeated them, and took the sphere?" I speculated.

"We did eventually catch up to them, but we weren't the ones to defeat them."

"Arbols," stated Hornet.

"Subterranean? Sub-arbols?"

Centaur nodded. "They were hairless, and pale. Their skin was almost translucent. But they were definitely arbols."

"If they didn't look like arbols...."

"They did, but didn't," Hornet attempted to explain. "They walked the same way. They had the same posture---and stature. Tall as a human, but skinnier. Lithe, not gaunt. And the way they spoke. Very fluid, like their communication was rehearsed, one word seamlessly flowing to the next."

"If they were the ones to defeat the trolls how were you able to collect the orb? Did they give it to you?"

"We took it while the trolls were engaged."

"They dropped it and we picked it up," Centaur clarified.

"And neither group had a problem with this?" I asked.

"Like I said, they were engaged," said Hornet, "the trolls *and* the sub-arbols."

"Neither wished to retrieve the orb after the battle?"

"We didn't stick around long enough to find out," said Centaur.

"Neither group seemed to pay too much attention to us," General Paint added. "Chaotics tend to be careless. I don't think the arbols were even aware of the orb."

"So, the sub-arbols didn't attack the trolls because of the orb?" I questioned.

"It was either to defend their territory or a preemptive strike."

"You think the sub-arbols have moved to the Dreadful Mountains, then? They weren't just passing through."

"They had to go somewhere," stated Hornet.

"So, it *was* the sub-arbols who built that tunnel? And the continuation of that tunnel led to...here?"

"Well...." Before Hornet could respond, Twig insisted I eat something.

"And here it is," said my host. Two minken walked into the room, one carrying a wooden bowl with some pale liquid in it, the other a small crystal platter with a thick slice of dark bread on it.

"You need to get your strength back," said Twig. "Without an energy healing elixir, you're going to have to recover the old fashion way."

"I apologize for not having any penta. Pulp understands my disdain for it. Most gents---unfortunately---employ it. Our identity correlates to our size, and the lack of changes to our appearance, not to us being able to fly or expel fire."

"I wasn't confident I could use penta," I declared. "There are tales of mutations countering their activation."

"Gents don't have that many mutations," Twig contended.

"Some have more. I believe my incompatibility was what almost killed me. It was like an allergic reaction, but instead of getting sick my energy was drained, to a nearly fatal level."

I took a bite of the bread. It was delicious. Full-bodied wasn't a word that was usually used to describe bread, but it fit this bread. I wasn't able to swallow it. My throat was still that dry. I took a swig of water, lubricating it enough for the bite to slide down. The soup was basically a broth, with small bits of meat floating in it. I used the wooden utensil that was thrust into it. It was a cross between a spoon and a ladle. The soup was hot, but not scalding. I was able to place the utensil in my mouth without having to blow on it first. The soup was delicious.

"Chicken?"

"Eagle." I spit out what was in my mouth. "I assure you that eagle was never your brother or cousin. When you believed it was chicken why did you think it couldn't have been a re-creation? Why must an eagle be considered to be majestic, and chicken a gastronomical staple? This particular eagle was picking on the minken. You pick on mine, you become soup."

"I must remember to never disturb you or the minken," Centaur commented.

"The unchanged are too much like gents for me to eat one. Those tales about gents eating people are made up to keep stupid people and infants from wandering out alone or at night."

"Gents never eat people? Even those in the Negative Frontier?"

"Only stupid people and infants."

As the soup and bread entered my body it felt like I was being fueled. My energy level improved dramatically. I slurped out the last bit of soup too deep to corral with the utensil. "Sorry."

"Don't be." Lord Bruin took the bowl and platter from me. He handed them to the minken. They rushed off. "You're in the Chaotic Frontier. Traditions don't hold up too well here."

"You were about to confirm who built that tunnel."

"Speculation was confirmed," said Hornet. "We took a wrong turn somewhere...."

I looked at General Paint.

"We travelled the most direct route," the trog proclaimed. "It just happened to pass through where the arbols were constructing the tunnel."

"General Paint forgot to share this detail with us," said Centaur.

"Individuals are too small to be perceived."

"And the tunnel?"

"It's usually quicker to travel through larger corridors."

"Fortunately, no one noticed us, or if they did they didn't feel we were enough of a threat to challenge us."

"The construction was fascinating," spoke Hornet enthusiastically.

"It was an abomination," General Paint countered. "They didn't use a pick and axe."

"They sprayed a liquid, which softened the stone, enough that shovels were sufficient to excavate. That wasn't even the best part. Instead of using ore carts or bags to haul off the debris, animals were employed, but instead of pulling or dragging they carried, internally---they consumed the ore. They must have weighed quite a bit by the time they became full. Their eight legs were stout, like an elephant's. Their bodies were elongated like a worm. Their mouths were enormous, almost as large as their heads. They didn't appear to have any eyes, so they must have perceived by sound and vibration."

"Where did they take the stone?" I asked. "To the surface? How did they expel it? Do I want to know?"

General Paint grimaced.

"You probably don't, but I'm still going to tell you," Hornet continued. "As we resumed our return to you we stumbled onto another of those...I guess you would call them barracks---a large cavern with dozens of buildings that looked like mushrooms. One of these buildings was under construction. Apparently, digested rock makes good building material."

"It was vomited?"

"Excreted."

"So, these sub-arbols make them homes out of…."

"Feek."

"It must have really smelled in there."

"Earthy."

"Whatever matter was mixed with the rocks during the digestion process must have also been inorganic," Centaur conjectured.

"And no one noticed you, again?" I asked.

"Apparently not."

"Very undisciplined," General Paint grunted.

"If may be that they just didn't care," Twig hypothesized. "The powerful become cocky."

"A weakness we may use to our advantage one day."

"That's one way of looking at it," said Centaur. "Another is whatever the sub-arbols are up to they are too powerful to not succeed."

"It won't matter if we can escape this planet," Hornet reminded us. "Let's see where that last sphere is."

"I'm curious about something," Twig declared. "Why build tracks here? I can understand someone wanting to invade Gulag or Rhinopolis, or even Kenwood, but why the Dreadful Mountains? There's nothing here."

"Troops," General Paint said matter-of-factly.

"Trolls and ogres for troops?" Centaur questioned.

"It wouldn't be my first choice…or second…or third. A hypothesis, not a validation."

"Directing chaotics is like herding cats," I stated, "entertaining, but not very constructive. If I were to choose something nasty to fight for me I would be heading to the Grim

Mountains. The creatures there are more disciplined in their brutality."

"Who says they aren't exploiting both?" Hornet questioned.

He gathered the five spheres. With Centaur's and General Paint's assistance they were connected. With the portal missing just one of its segments, the pieces stretched across a substantial portion of the room. Its diameter was between two and three meters. Hornet held onto the center sphere as Centaur and General Paint stood on contrasting sides of the bed holding the exterior orbs. The array wobbled. Hornet rotated around the room. Centaur and General Paint had difficulty keeping up. There were people in the way, mainly me, and a bed. For a brief instance the trog joined me. He tried not to gouge me with a knee or an elbow. He wasn't completely successful.

"What's going on?" I asked.

"It's moving." A moment later the contraption tilted up. Hornet had to let go or be lifted off his feet. "It's never done that before, or been that intense."

"We've never been short just one," said Centaur. For an instant the open end of the connected spheres was pointing to the ceiling, then it began to fall.

We ran outside, even I, who had enough of an adrenaline rush to make it to the drawbridge before I was drained. A large red drak was high in the sky, flying north. "It must have been directly overhead a moment ago," said Twig.

I held tightly onto an icy pillar as I studied the creature. Something drooped from its neck. "The sphere is tethered."

"It must be heading to the Grim Mountains," said Centaur. "Why is it moving around so much? Don't most creatures stay in their own territory? At least in their own frontier?"

"We don't," said Hornet.

"That's because we're on a mission."

"Maybe it's also on a mission."

"What mission might a drak be on?" asked Twig.

"It's prettee," said Sumac.

"Thank you for electing to live nearby," said Lord Bruin. "Too few can perceive the world as wondrously as you."

"HOW MANY TIMES ARE WE GOING TO HAVE TO CHASE THAT DRAK FROM ONE END OF LIMBO TO ANOTHER?!" General Paint had a calm demeanor unless something really riled him. When that pent-up fury erupted it was a wonder to behold.

"We have a visitor." Lord Bruin walked back into Ursa Major. We followed him to his private chambers on the third story. My weakness was severe enough I had to be helped up the two flights of stairs.

Chapter 28

A VISITOR

A lynx walked away from the transport portal. "LYNN!" Hornet looked shocked, then pleased, then perplexed. "Didn't you say we would be reunited on the Gold Coast?"

"Nice to see you too. Premonitions are based on current events. When events change, so does the future. How was I to know you were able to impregnate a woman? That anyone was able to." The cat rubbed its body against Hornet and Centaur. Compulsively, they petted it back.

"You know about Dinga?"

"Enough to know she will deliver in less than a week."

"That's impossible," stated Centaur. "She's only been pregnant for three. Isn't gestation normally 24 weeks?"

"Gaea has chosen to speed up the process. The child needs to be born now. The future of all of us depends upon it."

*** this concludes book 5 of the Limbo Chronicles ***

Appendix

GENT

Names of gent with year they were created (Limbo Calendar, year 0 being the metric year the penal colony was first inhabited), height and morality:

Titans – 8
Granite – 41 (6 meters) Neutral
Toe – 46 (7 meters) Chaotic-Positive
Lord Thump – 52 (3 meters) Chaotic-Negative
Lord Dung – 57 (5 meters) Chaotic-Negative
Scree – 63 (6 meters) Neutral
Fir – 69 (5 meters) Ordered-Positive
Toad & Stool – 74 (3 meters) Chaotic
Urchin – 79 (4 meters) Positive
Boulder – 83 (4 meters) Chaotic
Lord Coal – 91 (5 meters) Ordered-Negative
Jasmine – 94 (4 meters) Neutral
Lady Palm - 98 (4 meters) Negative
Lord Nettle – 102 (4 meters) Negative
Mist – 105 (5 meters) Neutral
Lord Bruin – 109 (5 meters) Chaotic-Negative
Pulp – 114 (3 meters) Chaotic-Positive
Lord Tick – 123 (2.5 meters) Chaotic-Negative
Lord Hide – 132 (3 meters) Ordered-Negative

DRAK

Names of drak, with year they were created (Limbo Calendar, year 0 being the metric year the penal colony was first inhabited):

Mac – 5 (deceased)
Nine-Talon – 12 (deceased)
Amber – 16 (deceased)
Sands – 17
Scar – 23 (deceased)
Bangle – 29 (deceased)
Lamprey – 34
Obsidian – 35
Thorn – 44
Nimbus – 54
Scorpion – 55
Gravity – 62
Fern – 66
Branch – 67
Puddle – 70
Flea – 72
Sequoia – 76
Berry – 80
Hail – 87
Grit – 88
Straw – 93
Algae – 99
Cactus – 105
Tar – 110
Dusk – 115
Silver – 122
Whittle - 127
Acorn - 129
Mirror - 132
Crystal - 136

TIME

The base unit for metric time is the second:

1 second = 1000 mils
1 minute = 100 seconds
1 hour = 100 minutes = 2:46:40 hours
1 day = 10 hours = 1:03:46:40 days
1 week = 10 days = 11:13:46:40 days
1 month = 10 weeks = 115:17:46:40 days
1 year = 10 months = 3:61:16 years
1 decade = 10 years = 31:251 years
1 century = 10 decades = 316:324 years

1 Limboan day = 8.64 metric hours
1 Limboan year = 316 metric days

RELIGION

Cor – Physical
Min – Mental
Fas – Emotional

CITIES AND TOWNS

Name and population, 142 metric years after the creation of Dartmoor. Location in percent degrees, and distance in kilometers from the center of the penal colony:

Gulag – 242000 – 00 – 000
Rhinopolis – 71000 – 65 – 790
Coolatta – 62000 – 67 – 370
Kenwood – 51000 – 89 – 930
Sunport – 46000 – 39 – 670
Capetown – 42000 – 09 – 350
Jasper – 31000 – 12 – 820
Grimboro – 23000 – 17 – 950
Topiary – 19000 – 48 – 570
Newport – 12000 – 96 – 820
Zephyr – 9900 – 08 – 100
Palm Desert – 9600 – 37 – 620
Penn – 9000 – 15 – 880
Berry – 8200 – 88 – 540
Norwood – 8000 – 04 – 840
Monkey Hill – 7700 – 06 – 210
Norport – 7500 – 09 – 780
Ingrid – 6500 – 13 – 280
Palm Dust – 6300 – 40 – 720
Lyco – 6200 – 65 – 930
St. Charles – 6100 – 49 – 820
Badlands City – 5800 – 41 – 790
Mula – 5100 – 92 – 900
Tarragon – 5000 – 41 – 670
Spruce – 4900 – 16 – 840
Sunset City – 4900 – 66 – 810
Three Rivers – 4600 – 64 – 550
Violet – 4600 – 87 – 430
Alexandria – 4600 – 24 – 710
Blowing Sand – 4400 – 09 – 840
Nine Palms – 3900 – 56 – 830
Drake – 3600 – 46 – 030
Carlton – 3400 – 15 – 130
Owlwood – 3400 – 87 – 750
Northern Roost – 3300 – 97 – 990
Port Royal – 3200 – 75 – 690
Salton – 3200 – 35 – 690
Wayward Gull – 2800 – 54 – 580
Port Moor – 2700 – 13 – 760
Reed – 2600 – 63 – 280
Seaview – 2500 – 46 – 790
Amber – 2400 – 42 – 900
Plymouth – 2300 – 48 – 400
Seawood – 2200 – 70 – 900
Sampson – 2100 – 47 – 930
Paradise – 2100 – 31 – 570
Charlie's Island – 2000 – 44 – 320
Typhoon – 2000 – 09 – 520
Filbert – 1700 – 95 – 410
Gargantuan – 1700 – 18 – 900
Spinecrest – 1200 – 04 – 820
Idyllic Wood – 1100 – 85 – 400

ELEM

Elem Aqua – Blue – Water **+**
Elem Fiero – Red – Fire **-**
Elem Terra – Green – Earth **^**
Elem Aero – Yellow – Air *****
Elem Essence – Black – Soul **#**

PENTA

Heal Flesh **++^++**
Heal Disease **++-++**
Heal Energy **++*++**
Water Elemental **++#++**
Fire Elemental **--#--**
Stone Elemental **^^#^^**
Air Elemental ****#****
Create ***^#^***
Animate ***^^^***
Transport ***+-+***
Enlarge **^^+^^**
Shrink **^+^+^**
Rise ****+****
Water Burst ***+^+***
Cold Burst ***-+-***
Hot Burst ***---***
Wind Burst ****^****
Electrical Burst ****-****
Air Barrier ***^^^***
Solid Barrier **^^*^^**
Soften **^+++^**
Harden **+^^^+**
Wind ****^****
Hail ***+^-***
Cold Front ***-+-***
Warm Front ***---***
Clouds ***^+^***
Sun ***-^-***
Snow ***+-+***
Rain ***+^+***

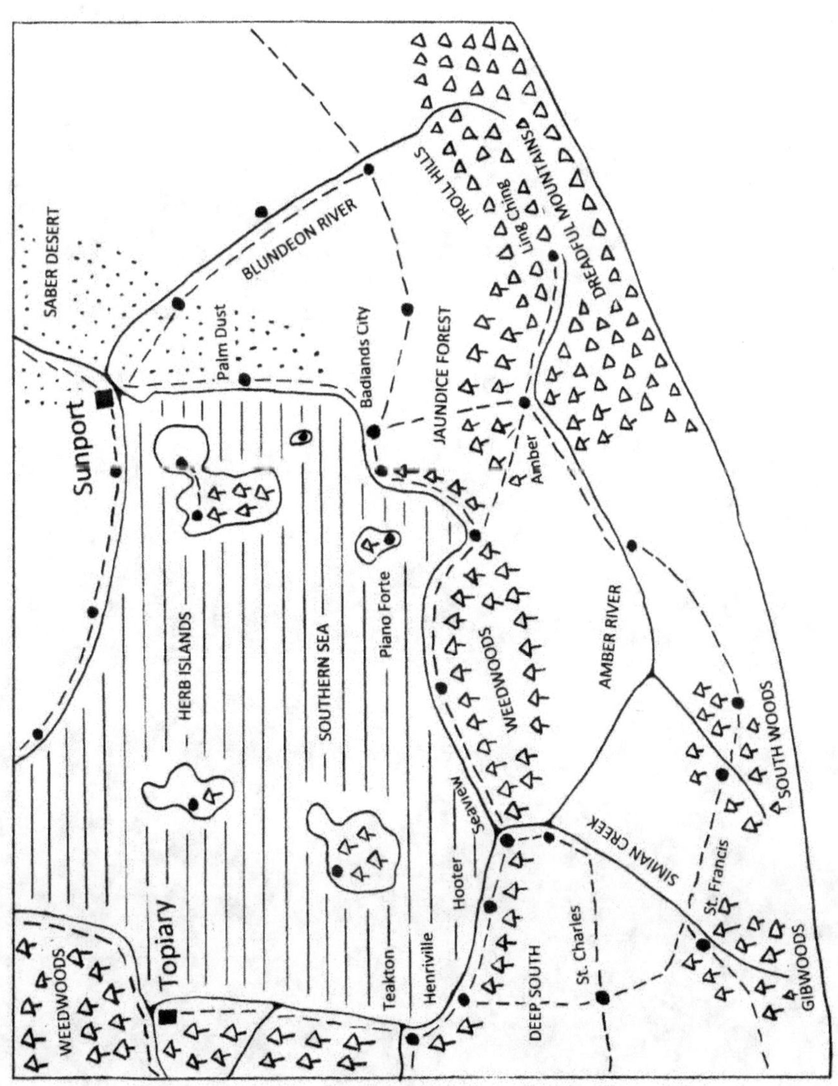
SABER DESERT
BLUNDEON RIVER
Palm Dust
Badlands City
TROLL HILLS
Ling Ching
DREADFUL MOUNTAINS
JAUNDICE FOREST
Amber
Sunport
HERB ISLANDS
SOUTHERN SEA
Piano Forte
WEEDWOODS
AMBER RIVER
SOUTH WOODS
SIMIAN CREEK
St. Francis
GIBWOODS
St. Charles
DEEP SOUTH
Seaview
Hooter
Henriville
Teakton
Topiary
WEEDWOODS

www.ingramcontent.com/pod-product-compliance
Lightning Source LLC
Chambersburg PA
CBHW071912220626
47052CB00002B/321

* 9 7 8 0 9 9 8 3 8 3 8 4 2 *